Locked In

To Paula and Paul and the
rest of Newham Writers Workshop

Published by Gideon Burrows t/a ngo.media,
75 Gurney Road, Stratford, E15 1SL

ALSO BY GIDEON BURROWS

Fiction

Portico: The Social Media Thriller

The Illustrator's Daughter

The Spiral

Future Shop

Locked In

Ninja of Light: Hako Ninja 1 (as G D Burrows)

Ninja of Steel: Hako Ninja 2 (as G D Burrows)

Non-fiction

Your Life In The Metaverse

Metaverse 101

Glioblastoma: A guide for patients and loved ones

Living Low Grade: A patient guide

This Book Won't Cure Your Cancer

Men Can Do It: Why Men Don't Do Childcare

Chilli Britain: A Hot and Fruity Adventure

Martin & Me

LOCKED IN

GIDEON BURROWS

May 2022

Chris,

Hope you enjoy the summer.

Best regards,

Gideon Burrows.

4/20

1

Pop!

Silence.

Piercing, ringing, ringing, ringing, ear piercing ringing, complete darkness.

...

"Hold on fella, wake up, oh shit, stay with me, HELP OVER HERE! Stay with me boy, I've got you, I've got you, what the hell? Someone, ambulance."

...

"Four, five, six, seven, eight, break, and one, two, three, four, five, six, seven, eight, break, and one, two, three, four..."

What? What's happening?

"Shall I take over mate?"

"Seven, eight, thanks, two, three, four, five, oh shit, where's the ambulance?"

"I'm a fire fighter, trained in CPR. Okay, here we go. And one, two, three, four. Get me a T-shirt. Cloth. Anything to stuff in the wounds. Five, six, seven, eight."

"Here, will this do?"

"Perfect. Okay, and one, two, three, four."

Screaming.

"Come on, boy."

Woo woo woo woo woo woo woo woo woo.

"No spectators, stand back. Go find help someone!"

Woo woo woo.

...

"Okay, going again, stand back, three, two, one," weeee-eeeeee, hmmmph, "continue CPR, warming up, and again ready to go, clear, three, two, one."

Weeee-eeeeee, hmmmph.

...

"Got him, Ceris, got him. That's it, come back to us, okay, wow, Jesus, flashers. Straight to St Michael's."

Slam, rumble, woo woo woo woo woo woo woo woo.

Silence.

"Stay with me."

Woo woo woo.

Silence.

Woo woo woo.

"He's fitting, Ceris. Pull over."

Wraw, wraw.

"Check vitals. Okay, sedation, 50ml, check..."

Woo woo.

"Stable, oh shit. Full flashers, Ceris. ICU, hold on lad, oh what a freaking mess, oh, hold on, we got you."

Silence.

Rattle, bang, clip, clip, clip, clip.

"ICU three"

Woo, woo.

Hello? Hello? What's happening?

"Other ambulances, casualties, maybe fifty, a bloody mess."

Clip, clip, clip, beep, bang.

"Okay, Doctor. Bay four, surgeon, nurse. Heavy bleeding. First responders stuffed major wound with a rainbow flag, thank God. Scissors, ventilator immediately."

Bump. Bump.

"You okay, Ceris?"

"Let's get back to Piccadilly, get the next one."

"Shit yeah. Well done."

"Good luck mate."

"He's going to need it. Long night ahead, long night. Cheers. More sedation, Nurse. This is real bad, sounds like it's a massacre down there, notify other hospitals. We're full already."

Silence.

Beep-beep.

Clink. Shuffle.

"Okay, Nurse, anaesthetist's report please?"

"2.5 mg/kg IV titrated, at approximately 40 mg every 10 seconds for 50 seconds."

"Blood loss?"

"Heavy, Doctor. "

"Thank you, please proceed."

"Okay, Doctor."

Hello? Help me? Please, someone.

Clink.

"And, wait. Okay, he's going under."

"Christ, what happened out there?"

Silence.

Silence.

Swish. Click.

Beep-beep.

"Any update, Nurse?"

"No Doctor. Pulse is stable and he's still breathing by himself. But no responses. Body shock coma, perhaps?"

"Let's hope so. Head wounds, we'll have to wait and see. Have neurology been informed?"

"Yes, Doctor. And neurosurgery are on standby."

"Is there an MRI planned?"

"We're waiting for neurology."

"Shit, what's the delay?"

"Lots of urgent cases, I imagine. How's it looking out there, Doctor?"

"Carnage. We've lost too many here in St Michael's. Six so far. Two on the brink. And this guy? Dozens more critically injured."

"He'll pull through. Good work, Doctor."

"Really?"

Silence.

"It's good of you to check on him, I guess time will tell."

"Keep me informed, Nurse."

"Of course."

Swish. Click.

Beep-beep. Ah. Beep-beep. Ah. Beep-beep.

Silence.

2

"Doctor Ann Atwan, general consultant, how can I help you?"

"Dillon Kendrick, acting on behalf of Westminster social services, but I'm also a forensic psychologist by profession. How is he?"

"Still in a coma and quite unstable. We've not been able to detect brain function yet, so he's not aware of us."

"No?"

"No sensations at all, as far as we can determine. Could be shock. The brain closing down to protect itself. Still, it's only been two days. We did a brain MRI and CT yesterday. Severe injury to the brain, but we've not been able to pin anything down neurologically. I'm not sure what you're doing here, to be honest?"

"I'm the responsible adult, Doctor. They say no family have come forward?"

"Not so far."

"Okay, so I'm to represent him as a vulnerable person on behalf of the council. As a possible victim of crime?"

"I see. Well, good luck with that."

"Doctor?"

"Well, look at the man. He has no senses. He's received serious internal and external injuries. He needs hospital treatment, not counselling. To my mind, he has a narrow chance of survival. If he's brain damaged, we could lose him any time."

"Can't he hear me?"

"No, he can't hear anything."

What?

"Doctor Atwan, I'm sorry, maybe I'm not getting this right. Before, I've only been responsible adult for, well errant teens at police stations. Anyway, I think I'm supposed to represent his interests in discussions with police and the medical establishment. Sorry, I'm not sure, I can check."

"The Medical Establishment?"

"Sorry, I didn't mean it that way. I want to be of help."

"Great. Then you can keep out of the way. Sure, sit here. Be responsible, if that's what the council want. Hopefully, a parent or partner will come forward before he dies."

"Thank you Doctor, I didn't mean to... And yes, let's hope so."

"Sorry, just busy. It's carnage out there. The less admin, the better."

"I understand."

Understand? I don't understand. Help me!

"You're just doing your job."

"And you, yours' Doctor. Thank you. And actually, I'm a volunteer. Like I say, mostly in the middle of the night, when some teenager gets arrested for possession and the parents won't come pick them up. For the fifth time that month. I'm totally out of my depth here, I'll be led by you."

"Okay, medical decisions default to the hospital."

"Of course, Doctor. I'm a psychologist, and there's not much to work with just now."

"Fine. It's a wait and see for the time being. We still have two on life support. Colleagues say they won't pull through. You acting for anyone else?"

"No, everyone else has a next of kin. Though there are some people missing, yet to report in as safe."

"A total tragedy."

"Yes, incredible. Thank you for what you're doing, Doctor."

"Thank you, Mr Kendrick."

"Oh, Doctor sorry? What are you calling him?"

"We're calling him David."

"David? My name is Dillon Kendrick and I'm a volunteer. I'm not sure if you can hear me?"

Silence.

"I've been asked by Westminster social services to act as your responsible adult. I hope you don't mind."

Hello?

"To be honest, I've not worked with anyone so, well, so incapacitated before. But I hope you'll find me a good advocate and I hope decent company until a next of kin is identified. The doctors are saying you have no senses at all."

Silence.

Hello? Hello, Dillon?

"Okay, this is weird. I guess they're assuming you have no control over your functions. Your sense of smell, taste, sight or hearing. Maybe you can't feel anything either? But hopefully somewhere in there you're alive. You have some serious injuries to heal. I'm sure you'll pull through."

I'm here, can you...

Silence.

"Oh, well, I don't know what else to say. You are in ICU. That's, er, isolated clinical unit. Is that right? Or critical unit? Wow, I don't know. I'll find out. And you have a heart monitor attached. And a feeding tube, going into your mouth. But that's it, really. Maybe that's all you need to know. I don't know. Sorry, it's all a bit weird. I'm not sure if you can hear me or if you can understand me or whether, frankly, I'm talking to you to make myself feel better.

"Anyway, I'm trying to do something. I've only really been responsible adult for kids before. You're possibly the victim of a crime, but no one has come to claim you, so you need a responsible person that's not a police officer or a doctor, so I guess that's me. It is my voluntary job and you need to know, David, that I'll do my best to look after your interests.

"I want to say to you David - well I know that's not your real name David - but I don't have anything else to call you just now. But what I want to say, is that, well, I'm really sorry this has happened to you. No-one knows what happened right now. Some say a gas pipe blew. Others are saying it was terrorists. Anyway, you don't need to hear all that. I'm not doing a very good job am I? So, I guess, I'll be here if the doctors need to make any big decisions."

Silence.

"Okay, I don't know what else to say. Shall we just sit here for a while?"

Oh God, please. I'm inside here.

Swish. Click.

"Oh, hello. Are you family?"

"Oh, no. Sorry. Erm."

"And you are?"

"I'm his responsible adult. Advocate?"

"Hello, I'm not sure what that is?"

"Dillon Kendrick. Here's my ID, from Westminster social services. I'm supposed to represent David, as responsible adult in lieu of next of kin. I'm a volunteer."

"Okay, yes. I understand. Anyway, I need to turn him a little. Bed sores, you know. And check his obs."

"Yes, of course, Nurse. Sorry, I know you have a name."

"Gail."

"Thank you, Gail. I should leave."

"No, that's fine."

"I'll stay, okay."

"Would you like a cup of tea?"

"Oh wow, yes. Just this once, I know you're not a... well a waitress. Thank you. I'm fine to help myself though?"

"It's fine, we appreciate what you volunteers do. It was a terrible tragedy."

"Yes, it was."

"Okay, I'll be along soon with your tea. Milk?"

"Milk, no sugar."

"Sure, thank you."

Swish. Click.

"I bet you'd like a cup of tea David? Well, the doctors are taking good care of you. And if they're not, I guess that's what I'm here for. To talk to the right people anyway. I'm just jabbering on.

"I hope I'm not keeping you awake. I'm sorry, I can't tell because your eyes are closed. Maybe you can't even hear me. To be honest, I feel a little out of my depth. Anyway, I'm Dillon and I've been talking too long. I'll shut up now.

Swish. Click.

"Oh, Gail, thank you. Oh, can I help?"

"No, I'm fine. Just *shifting* him. And now... okay, that's all I need."

"Thank you."

"No problem. Have a good morning."

"I will. Thanks again for the tea."

Swish. Click.

Silence.

3

Beep-beep.

What's that? HELLO!??

Beep-beep.

A noise? What is this?

Beep. Ah. Beep. Beep.

I'm alive. Thank you. Thank you.

Beep.

Thank you.

"David? David, what's going on? Nurse?"

Beep-beep-beep-beep. Beep-beep-beep-beep.

What's happening?

Beep-beep-beep-beep-beep-beep-beep-beep.

Hello? Hello? I can't breath. Help me! Help me!

"Oh, fuck. Shit. Hit the button. Where is it? Here, the button. Orange? That's not right. Fuck. David? David? Nurse!"

Beep-beep-beep-beep-beep-beep-beep-beep.

"Fuck it. Orange."

Ring. Ring. Ring.

Beep...

"David, oh shit, stay with me... Nurse? NURSE!"

Beep...

...

...

...

"Elephant."

...

...

"Circus. Off she went."

...

...

"Trump, trump, trump."

"What can I do, Nurse?"

"Hit that red button."

"Red?"

Whah. Whah. Whah.

"That's it, come on David. The head of the herd was calling..."

Swish. Click.

"How long, Nurse?"

"Three minutes at least, Doctor Atwan. My arms are wrecked."

"Give me 30 more seconds?"

"Can I help?"

"Yes, continue the rhythm. Press here. Nelly the elephant packed her trunk, and said goodbye to the circus."

...

"Okay, Nurse, machine ready, prepare to stand clear."

Whee-eeeee

"From far far away."

Beep.

"Ready to clear, Nurse Gail?"

"Wait, Doctor."

"Nurse? I said, are you ready to clear?"

"Doctor, I think Mr Kendrick has got him."

Beep. Beep.

...

"You sure, Nurse?"

"Five seconds more?"

Beep. Beep. Beep.

"There... Bloody hell, he's back."

"Oh my God."

"You got him, Dillon. You got him."

"Oh, my God. Is he back?"

"Yes, you saved him."

"No, I pressed the wrong button."

"You saved him Dillon."

"You both did. Many wouldn't have. Nurse, you'll have to decompress after this. Mr Kendrick, are you okay?"

"Yes, yes. I just can't... I mean, wow. Thank you Doctor."

Silence.

"Wait. Will he be okay? I mean, that was a long time without oxygen?"

"What did we have, Nurse?"

"Four minutes? Four-thirty. If I got that right?"

"Then I suspect so. People have come back after much longer. We'll have to see. There's a possibility of brain damage, maybe permanent scarring? But no more than he might have gained from the explosion in the first place. Really, both of you. Well done. You made a difference today.

"I better go and write this up. Nurse Gail, I'll need your signature."

"Yes, Doctor. Can I have a moment?"

"Of course, take as long as you need."

Crying.

Swish. Click.

"Are you okay, Nurse?"

"Yes, yes, Dillon. It's just the shock. Sorry, very unprofessional of me."

"It's quite okay, Nurse. It's enough for anyone. Here, take a seat. Water?"

"Thanks."

"Wow."

"Mr Kendrick, you saved his life. There's something special going on there. That's three times he's gone under."

"Honestly, I had no idea what I was doing. Will he come round?"

"We did what we could. If he had even a little life left in him, I suspect that's all gone after that. Nearly five minutes with no oxygen? I know my bloods, Mr Kendrick."

"I guess we just wait then?"

"Yes Mr Kendrick, we just wait."

Rolling, rolling. Bumping. Bumping.

Where are the sirens? I can't hear them. Take me to hospital, quickly, take me. Am I hurt? Talk to me.

I'm alive. Don't let me die. I'm alive. God help me, I'm alive. HELP ME!

Rolling, rolling. Bumping. Bumping.

Oh God, I feel. I feel sick. But in my head. I don't feel my body. I don't feel the rolling. I don't feel the bumping.

It's in my head. Am I dead?

I don't feel. But I feel. I hear, so I feel.

Bump.

Please help me. The ambulance is gone. There are no sirens.

I don't feel, but I can hear. I can hear moving. Where am I going? Where are you taking me?

Oh God, I'm dead? Please HELP ME!

If I can hear, then I'm alive. Isn't that right?

There has to be me, to hear. If there wasn't me, there would be no sound.

Bump.

It's okay. The bed. I can hear the bed. The wheels rolling.

Bump.

The bed. Against the doors. Swish. Bang.

I can hear. I am alive, because I can hear. I feel really sick. I'm going to be sick.

Swish.

Comforting. The sound of life. The sound of me, alive.

Wait. Hello. Can you hear me? Help me. Please, can you hear me? Don't leave me. Help, help, HELP!

I'm here. Can't you hear me? Oh, shit. I can't take this. Help me! Why won't somebody help me?

Swish.

Swish. Click.

Silence.

Hello?

4

Good morning and welcome to Express News with me, Sophie Horgan.

The devastating explosion that went off during London's LGBTQ plus Pride Festival on Saturday is suspected to have killed 11 people, and critically injured more than 100 others.

The Prime Minister has expressed her deepest sympathy for the victims, families, those at the parade and the wider LGBTQ plus community.

One man remains in a serious critical condition at St Michael's hospital, having been in a coma since the explosion.

Our correspondent Dean Joyce is at the site of the explosion, close to Piccadilly Circus in the centre of London.

Thank you, Sophie. Yes, doctors at St Michael's have said they are doing everything they can to assist the man. They say they are working with the Metropolitan Police to identify him, and have asked anyone who may not have heard from a loved one since the Pride parade to get in touch.

A Metropolitan Police spokesperson said they are also examining CCTV footage closely for any reason for the explosion. The incident took place here, close to the Eros statue, around half-way through the parade as a crowd of Black Lives Matter campaigners were passing the famous London landmark. Police are appealing for mobile phone footage of the day, as they attempt to build a picture of what happened.

Police have urged the public not to jump to conclusions about the cause of the explosion, but sources say there may have been some gas repair works taking place close to the scene of the incident here, around 2pm on Saturday. They have urged the public to keep speculation to a minimum, saying they will not hesitate to prosecute false accusations and hate speech as a result of the events.

Back to you Sophie.

That was Dean Joyce, reporting live from Piccadilly Circus. A helpline has been established for families who are are still concerned about loved ones who have not been in touch since the explosion. That number is...

Swish. Click.

It's a door! A door. That's what that sound is. Swish. Click. The door to a room. My room.

"Oh David, who's put the TV on like that?"

That voice again. Hello? Can you hear me?

"How crass. You don't need to be hearing any of that rubbish. It's all speculation, best you concentrate on getting better."

Hello, can you hear me? HELLO!

"David, I hope you don't mind. I read some research that said I should speak to you. Even if you can't hear me, the rhythm might sooth you."

Hello. Speak to me. I'm in here. Please, hear me.

"I read that if you recognise something I say, it might even jolt you back to life. I don't know, after what happened but, well."

Oh fuck. I'm alive in here! Help me. Please, hear me? I can't move. I can't see. Can you hear me?

"It took an age for me to find you. I didn't know they'd moved you off ICU. That's great news. One step at... Anyway, we're getting better, aren't we? I hear the police are coming in to see you today?"

Dillon? Is that your name. I'm not sure. Dillon, is that it?

"That'll be something different and I'm here to speak on your behalf. Should be pretty straight forward.

"Sorry David, no family member has come forward yet. There's still lots of missing people, people unaccounted for. Maybe your folks are on holiday or something? Oh, I wish I could help you."

David? Who is David? Can you help me? Hear me, Dillon! Hear me! I'm shouting. I'm fucking SHOUTING.

"Okay, I'm going to take a seat. I hope you don't mind. I guess I don't know much about you, and I'm not supposed to share much about myself because, well, this is all supposed to be about you."

What happened to me? Please, tell me the truth. What is this explosion?

"To be honest, I'm in a bit of a fluster. You see, I usually bring some magazines or some sweets, to bring the kid on side you know? Then they trust me when the police come with their questions.

"I wonder what you're into David? What magazine should I have brought for you? I'm thinking, not fast cars, football or gaming - that's what I'd bring for all the kids in the police station. They were all boys of course. There's nothing worse than a bored teenage boy in a police cell. No cigarettes allowed. Definitely no dope. I don't know much about football either, but I nod my head as if I do.

"So, let me see. A gay magazine? Nah, sorry David. You're

more than just gay. Fashion? Well, a bit uncomfortable, given your condition. Let's settle with bread making. I bet you make bread. I'll bring you a cooking magazine, how does that sound?"

Hello? Can you hear me? Cooking sounds good. Oh, I'd love to eat something just now. Hold on, am I alive? Can I eat? Can I smell? Touch me. Let me feel something? Please, give me some contact.

"Ah, maybe not. See, stereotypes trip you up over this kind of thing. You're probably some brain surgeon or something, or some super scientist. I'm aiming way low with the cookery. How about New Scientist? Scientific American? Now, I've got to be thinking New Statesman rather than The Spectator. God help us if not. Sorry, rather judgemental of me. And now I'm waffling. Again."

The Sun, Daily Mail. Dad says those are real papers. The Guardian? Don't bring that trash into my house.

"Listen, I'm going to go and get a coffee. And I promise, I'll pick up a magazine at random. Just a thought, I could read it out to you."

No, don't go. Help me out of this. I'm scared. I need you to be with me.

"Now, don't you be going anywhere, David. I'll be back before the doctors arrive. I'll see you in a short while. And I'll tell those orderlies to keep that TV off."

No, I want to know. What happened? Kind man, please, don't leave me alone.

Chanting. Rhythmic chanting.

Human voices. Angry voices.

Bung-bung, bung-bung-bung.

Bung-bung, bung-bung-bung.

Familiar, but strange.

Voices.

Drums?

Bung-bung, bung-bung-bung.

Bung-bung, bung-bung-bung.

No. NO!

Bung-bung, bung-bung-bung.

Bung-bung, bung-bung-bung.

Before. Before.

Chanting. Shouting. Is it? Is it praying?

Bung-bung, bung-bung-bung.

Counting down.

Bung-bung, bung-bung-bung.

Any time now, it will go. Something terrible is going to happen.

Help me.

My feet. My feet. Oh, please stop. Not my, my feet. The agony. Please no. Jesus, please stop.

Bung-bung, bung-bung-bung.

Oh my God, any time now.

Bung-bung, bung-bung-bung.

Getting quicker.

Bung-bung-bung-bung-bung-bung-bung.

Beep. Beep. Beep.

Oh fuck. Too late. Close eyes. Close eyes tight. Burning heat. Get ready for the pain.

Silence.

No, the pain. Please! The heat. The searing. The blisters.

Wait.

Beep. Beep. Beep.

Gentle. Rhythmic.

It's not drums. Oh, God, it's not the drums.

Where am I?

Hospital noise.

Hospital.

Bung, bung, bung-bung-bung.

Quieter now. A heating system? Airflow. A fan, just catching. Going round.

Bung, bung, bung-bung-bung.

Beep. Beep. Beep.

Hospital noise. Oh thank you, hospital noise.

Let me listen.

Bung, bung, bung, beep, beep, beep.

A little comfort. The sounds are my friends. My only friends.

I am so afraid. So lonely. Somebody help me!

Swish. Click.

"Hello, okay we'll keep this short. I'm Detective Chief Inspector Philippa Pierce and this is my colleague Detective Inspector Kat Ling. And you are?"

Hello? Hello! Can you hear me?

"Dillon Kendrick, officer."

"You can call me DCI Pierce."

"Of course."

"And who do we have here? A John Doe?"

"He's been named as David, DCI Pierce. No relatives have yet been identified. No partner. No boyfriend. No husband."

Boyfriend? Husband?

"Okay, so who are you?"

"Responsible adult."

"Oh great, responsible adult. I'm looking at this guy and I'm feeling he's over eighteen."

"Yes, but he's classed as vulnerable, and a victim of crime."

"Okay, Mr Kendrick. *Possible* victim of a crime. You're welcome to observe or leave."

"I'm really sorry, Ma'am. Maybe I need to check, but I think it is my right to be here. And his right also?"

"I'm sorry?"

"Forgive me, Detective Chief Inspector, but I'm legally obliged by Westminster social services to be here at any contact with police or doctors or any other services. For David. I might have got that wrong. It's my first case of this type."

"Like I say, you're welcome to observe."

"Sorry, Ma'am. Like I say, I might have got it wrong, but - at least with the kids I work with - it not just an observational capacity. It is my legal obligation to protect the patient's wellbeing and interests."

"Give me strength. DI Ling, can you explain to me what's going on?"

"Sorry, Ma'am, I believe the patient has a right to independent representation as a possible victim of crime, because he is vulnerable."

"That man can't speak or move. What are we going to do, torture him?"

"DCI Pierce, I'm sorry, it would be a legal matter. We'd have to apply to a judge to have Mr Kendrick removed."

"Fine, fine. If we're going to be fussy. I suspect we're not going to be getting much out of David today by the looks of him. Could you take a note of Mr Kendrick and his role in this case?"

"Sure, Ma'am."

"DCI Pierce?"

"Yes, what is it now Mr Kendrick?"

"Sorry, don't want to overstep my remit, but, if you don't mind. May I say, well, perhaps there should be a little more decorum around David. He's a victim of a serious crime here."

"*Suspected* crime, Mr Kendrick. And from what I can see, there's no one at home. And given what I've been told by doctors, we can pretty much mark him down as a fatal casualty."

Oh, my God, Dillon? Am I going to die?

"The doctors are saying to me, Ma'am, there's a chance of recovery."

"Okay, so we'll pose some questions to him shall we Mr Kendrick?"

"I'm just doing my job, Ma'am."

"And I'm trying to do mine. Have you seen what it was like down there at Piccadilly Circus? Absolute mayhem. I'm just trying to identify the victims and those who've disappeared and trying to piece together what happened."

"Yes, I understand Ma'am. Sorry."

"Okay, let's start again. Mr Kendrick I apologise for any discourtesy. I've seen and heard some harrowing stuff over the last few days."

"Yes, sorry. Let me introduce you to David properly. My understanding is he has no senses currently. But there is a chance that he's still sentient. The doctors tell me he definitely can't see and he's paralysed with no movement detected whatever, including any sense of hearing. I think it's more of a brain thing."

"Okay, thank you, Mr Kendrick. A brain thing. Can he hear me?"

"I don't think so, no."

Yes. Yes I can. Please, can you hear me?

"Right. So, okay, as David's responsible adult, do you consider him sentient?"

"What do you mean?

"What I mean is, I'd like to pose some questions to David to establish where he was, how he got injured, what friends he was with, and anything we can use to trace a next of kin."

"I don't think he's capable of that. I've not had any response from David since I met him yesterday."

"Like I say, no one home. Mr Kendrick, do you know anything else about the patient? Apart from the medical records that have been taken since he came in?"

"Sorry, no."

"Okay, I think that's all we need for now. We've some other patients on the ward to speak to."

"Thank you officers."

"Don't mention it."

Door.

"Sorry David. What an awful woman. I'll be back tomorrow."

Wait don't go. I can hear you. You're Dillon. Dillon Kendrick. Please don't go.

Shuffle. Shuffle.

Please, don't go. What was this explosion? Please help me. I'm not gay. I wasn't at that parade. Football? I remember now, I was playing football. I don't understand.

Door.

Please, what happened to me? I'm alive. Is anyone there? I can't feel anything.

5

Silence

BANG!

Oh my God, oh my God. The heat. Oh, the pain. Help me. HELP ME!

BANG.

Oh no, I'm on the floor, I can't feel my legs. My head. Screaming. Lights flashing.

BANG!

My legs. My legs. Please, not that pain. Anything but that pain again.

BANG!

No, wait. It's different.

BANG!

Oh my God.

BANG!

Rhythmic. Wait, just for a moment...

BANG!

There is is again. No pain. No burning.

BANG!

I'm not screaming.

Bzzzz.

Bzzzz.

Whirring.

BANG!

Shouting? But not the same. Not the same as...

BANG!

No burning. No screaming. No smashed glass. No head pain. My wrists, my hands. No pain.

BANG!

It's outside. The window. Below.

BANG!

Bzzzz.

Bzzzz.

Could it be road works? A car, its engine?

BANG!

Quieter. No, not the same at all. Not even similar.

BANG!

A welcoming sound. Expected.

BANG!

Rhythm. Time passes with every sound.

BANG!

Exactly. Road noise. Street noise.

I can hear. I can make sense of the noise now. Voices. Sounds. I can tell the difference. Oh, thank God. I'm recovering. I'm coming alive.

No more pain. No danger of pain. I'm free.

I understand. I'm alive.

Bzzzz.

Bzzzz.

Comforting noise. Nothing sudden. Nothing scary. No panic. Lulls you back to...

Sleep.

"Ah David, good morning. Just in to open your curtains properly. Come on Sheila, let's get him turned so we can change his sheets. Hit the TV there, can you? Okay, we're going to just lift."

Welcome back to the Express News show, I'm Sophie Horgan.

And this morning, police have appealed for calm among the LGBTQ plus community as they revealed they are now treating the explosion at the London Pride Festival as an attack by terrorists, rather than the gas leak explosion they had originally suspected.

The Chief Executive of the LGBTQ plus organisation Out There, Dame Patricia Peters, has accused the police of delay that could be putting more members of the gay community at risk.

'We have been told for four days that it was probably a gas explosion, despite social media posts that show footage of the explosion taking place inside the crowd. It is time for the Metropolitan Police to act to reassure our community that we are safe, and to implement measures around London and beyond to prevent copycat attacks. The delay in announcing their suspicions has put LGBTQ plus people everywhere at risk.'

We turn to our correspondent Dean Joyce, who is at New Scotland Yard today.

Yes, Sophie.

The head of the Metropolitan Police, Gavin Wittacker, gave a short press conference this morning, stating that the nature of people's injuries indicated a bomb or bombs placed in the centre of the crowd.

He said a gas pipe explosion had now been ruled out.

The bombing is reminiscent, said one source, of the 1999

bombing of the Admiral Duncan pub on London's Old Compton Street, as well as attacks on London's ethnically diverse community at Brixton in South London and Brick Lane. Right wing extremist David Copeland is serving a life sentence as a result of the bombing campaign, which injured dozens, and killed three.

Police say they have particular interest in a green rucksack, which they would like to exclude from their enquiries.

"Well, will you look at that Sheila. They're saying it was a terrorist attack, for God's sake."

"Yeah, I heard that, Marjorie. Right by the Black Lives Matter banner. Disgusting, as if your people haven't had a hard time enough."

"I know and the gays too. You'd think the police should have had the terrorists in sight? I mean Black Lives Matter at a gay parade. I know the answer to two and two, Sheila. Even I could have made that connection."

"The Piccadilly Bomber they're calling him, aren't they, Marj?"

"Always got to have a name for them, don't they?"

Thank you Dean Joyce, our special correspondent reporting from Scotland Yard.

In related news, one man remains in a coma as a result of the Pride bombing. Police have not named him but have emphasised that the helpline for victims and families is still open.

Officers say they are still waiting to fully identify all those who were close to Piccadilly Circus at the time of the bombing. They are still appealing for any mobile phone footage, and for witnesses to step forward.

"That's it David, and we'll just move you back over here. Marjorie if you can thanks."

"That's great."

"Looks like you're big news, David. Such a shame no one has been in touch about you yet. But I'm sure they'll come."

"Poor parents."

"Yes, and sisters and brothers."

"You'd think, Sheila, someone would have been in touch? Such a shame."

"Okay David, that's you for now. We'll come back to give you a bed bath later this afternoon."

"Do you think that's ok?"

"What's that Marjorie?"

"Well, you know with him being gay? Shouldn't he have a man doing his bed bath?"

"That's ridiculous, Marj."

Wait? Gay? I'm not gay. Can you hear me? I'm not gay.

"He might prefer it, Sheila."

"He's not in any state to prefer anything."

"We should just get our job done."

"Don't you wonder though?"

"What, wonder what the gays like?"

"What it's like to be gay? I have a friend who's gay. She says she's always felt that way."

"Yeah, but maybe its different for women. It must be hard for a man. I mean so much is expected of a man to be tough and stuff."

"Well, this David seems tough enough. Nice body."

"Sheila!"

"That's not what I meant. Anyway, he sure must have been tough to get out there at that march and be proud of what he is."

I was at football. I didn't go to that parade.

"He might look vulnerable now, but I've seen the lovely bodies of some of those gays."

"Oh Sheila, you shouldn't say that. Come on by David, we'll see you this evening."

"Can't wait."

"Sheila that's not appropriate. We'll leave the TV on for you David. Something to listen to."

Door.

Our political editor Natasha Harding has been following the story closely, and reports now from Westminster.

Thank you, Sophie.

The Home Secretary, Francis Gardiner said last night in the House of Commons that he extended his deepest sympathies to those who had lost their lives and been victims of the attack.

He also expressed personal sympathy to the Saudi royal family, after they reported that a cousin of the current Minister of Defence, and member of the Saudi royals, was killed in the explosion. Two of his aides were seriously injured.

The Prince, Yusuf Al-Ghamdi, was said to be shopping close to Piccadilly Circus when the explosion took place. He died from his injuries at Southfields Hospital on Sunday morning, where his aides are said to be recovering.

British government diplomats said they are in touch with their Saudi counterparts, to express Her Majesty The Queen's condolences.

Mr Gardiner said he would back the Metropolitan Police with whatever emergency powers they needed to bring the perpetrators to justice.

Thank you, Natasha Harding.

In other news the Department for Environment have expressed the concern about rising CO2 levels on the A406 circular road ...

Silence.

Wait, I don't understand. Hello, are you there? I'm not gay. What's going on. Please help me.

"Hi David, it's me. Hope they've been looking after you."

Dillon?

Click.

"Why do they keep leaving the TV on for you, David? You don't want to hear about the explosion. At least they could put on a music channel or something."

I do want to hear. Why was I there? I'm trying to remember. Oh, God, what happened to me?

"Anyway, I brought a copy of The Times today. Middlish - shouldn't offend any of us. I've brought my coffee in too, I hope you don't mind. Now, let's skip over the first few pages, just the usual about the, well, you don't want to hear about that - and, well, here we go: about whales being spotted off the coast of Newcastle. I do like whales and dolphins, David. So, here goes."

Knock.

Door.

"Ah hello, Doctor Atwan. Nurse Gail. Good to see you both."

"You too, Mr Kendrick."

"How is David today? Have the nurses been looking after him?"

"It seems so, but someone keeps leaving the TV on the news. I'm not sure that's appropriate. I've brought him in something else to read. Well, for me to read to him."

"Quite so. Nurse can you ensure that doesn't happen?"

"Of course, Doctor. Though we're assuming he has no hearing?"

Different voice. Woman's voice.

I can tell now. Different voices. Let me see.

"I don't think we can assume anything at this stage. Now, Mr Kendrick."

Yes, that's the doctor. Doctor Atwan.

"Please, call me Dillon."

"Dillon then. I hear the police came in to see David?"

It was the doctor. Doctor Atwan. Ann Atwan. I'm getting this.

"Just routine, they said. I had to remind them of my position."

"Yes, they're desperate just now."

Another voice. That's the nurse. Nurse Gail.

"The public is breathing down their neck and social media is going wild. There have been some protests. Black Lives Matter and LGBTQ plus rights together. There's one outside this hospital."

It was Nurse Gail.

So, Nurse Gail. Doctor Atwan. And Dillon. Always Dillon.

"What, a protest?" *It was Doctor Atwan.*

"No, a vigil." *It was Nurse Gail.*

"For the victims of the bombing still here at St Michael's. I saw a banner, 'Hope for David'. " *It was Dillon.*

"Oh, that's good."

"Well, as long as they don't get in the way of hospital business." *It was Doctor Atwan.*

"The police have set up an area for them to hold their vigil. Some of them are staying overnight."

"What on hospital property?"

"Wouldn't you do the same if the hospital had been attacked?"

"Do they know his real state?"

"Only what the police have released, and the papers are

speculating. To their mind he's in a coma. That's enough for now. We're not releasing anything else."

"Do they think he'll recover? Do you?"

"I don't want to speculate, Mr Kendrick."

"My brother is gay, Doctor." *It was Nurse Gail.* "He says the community is just totally cut up by what happened. I mean Pride is supposed to be a celebration. Not really any longer a protest for rights."

"Are the police thinking it might be race related? Didn't the bomb go off close to the Black Lives Matter banners?" *It was Dillon.*

"Speculation. Thank you Nurse. Nurse pass me my torch, okay left eye unresponsive to light and right okay same. Okay, we'll test hearing next."

Click.

Click.

I can hear you Doctor! I need you to know I can hear you clicking your fingers.

"Left ear shows no physical response to sound and..."

Click.

Click.

"Right also negative. And the needle please."

Yes, right too. I can hear you!

"Doctor."

"Thank you Nurse. Okay, the needle right knee no response and left outer thigh, no response. And just for good measure, Nurse, if you would."

No. No feeling.

"Of course."

"Together, one, two, three, pulling up. And needle at back of neck. No physical response, and slowly release. Okay, well, I think we can conclude there is no response physically to any stimuli."

You're wrong, Doctor. I can hear you. I can't feel, but I can hear.

"I'd like to put him under the CT scan again and run the same tests as last time. Let's see if we can get any brain activity. Nurse can you see to that please?"

"Emergency?" *It was Nurse Gail.*

"No not an emergency. We'll have to get in the queue. David won't be going anywhere quickly."

"Do you think he'll ever get some feeling back?" *It was Dillon. He has such a lovely voice. Caring.*

"We don't know Mr Kendrick, I've only seen a few cases of this syndrome. In many they do eventually recover some sensation. Even the slightest movement can open them up from the inside out. He could be fully conscious in there, but I think it's unlikely."

I AM! Please, Dillon. Tell them I am. I'm here. Please, help me.

"It is just as likely that his brain injury was so severe there's no memory or intelligence or self-awareness in there at all. His bodily functions are still working, but the self-conscious brain might be entirely gone."

"We have to wait longer to do many more tests." *It was Nurse Gail.*

"David needs to recover from his injuries as best he can. There's a huge shock element to all of this. His brain could have shut his functions down with the trauma. We may see something over the next week or so but, like I say, I'll get him into a CAT scanner and we'll take another look."

"Do you think he's in pain?"

"You saw, Mr Kendrick. There was no physical reaction to my needle so it's very unlikely he can feel any of the damage that his body suffered. Head. Legs. Hands. The shards into his face and obviously the damaged brain."

No, Dillon. It's okay. I feel nothing.

"Let's hope not."

"Yes, Gail, let's hope not. We have him on some low dose pain killers in case he comes round and suddenly goes into a pain shock. But otherwise let's assume he's without any senses at all."

NO! I can hear you. Touch me. Squeeze my hand. Make me react.

"Okay, I'll leave you to it. Thank you David. Mr Kendrick. Nurse Gail can you get on with booking that CAT scan?"

"Yes, certainly Doctor."

Door.

"Poor man. Any sign of any next of kin as yet?" *It was Dillon.*

"No, it's strange. Everyone else has come to the hospital. We've dealt with them. You'd think there would be someone, a family member, a boyfriend?" *It was Nurse Gail.*

Why do people keep saying boyfriend?

"Do you think it's worth my talking to the group outside? Thank them for the support, on David's behalf?" *It was Dillon.*

"Seems to me they're very wary of talking to anyone. Even the police."

"I could give it a try. See if anyone actually knows David? We don't know how bothered the police are if they don't think he'll come round. I saw them in here. Going through the motions."

"Well, if you're happy enough, Mr Kendrick, I need to change David just now."

"Yes, of course. See you later David. Hope to be back tomorrow. Goodbye Gail."

Oh, Dillon. Don't go. Will you stay? I'm so lonely.

Door.
Silence
"Right, David, let's get you stripped."
Click.

... The Metropolitan Police have said investigations into the Piccadilly bomb show a green rucksack remains the centre of their enquiries. It could be a significant clue to who carried out the bombing.

Our special correspondent, Dean Joyce reports.

Thank you, Sophie. That's right: the police are attempting to track the journey of the rucksack to Piccadilly Circus on Saturday. They have now specifically appealed for mobile phone footage from the scene, as well as from travellers to the parade, who may have captured a picture of the rucksack.

This photograph has been provided. It is said to be a deep green medium sized bag, with two shoulder straps, from the retailer Bigfoot. The retailer has provided a sample of the bag to police, so they can look for an exact match.

Thank you Dean Joyce. Now, *our political editor, Natasha Harding, reports on the political situation regarding the bombing.*

Yes, the Saudi royal family have now publicly stated that relations with Britain are 'delicate' and their special relationship with the government is at risk.

Officials are questioning why police resources were not used more effectively to prevent the death of Saudi royal family member, Prince Yusuf Al-Ghamdi, who was said to be shopping close to Piccadilly Circus when the explosion took place. The Foreign Secretary is said to be writing officially...

"That's you David. See you soon."

There is noise all around me, but there is nothing but silence in my head.

I can separate the sounds now. The object from the sound. I know there is a trolley juddering as it runs down a corridor. But I feel nothing, no vibrations, I see no shadows passing.

It is noisy. But there is no life.

Voices. There are a hundred voices. Men, women, officials, crying, joy, shouting, whispering. But they all sound the same. They are noise, lots of noise, noise so loud and varied, yet so equal.

They are silent.

There are rings, and beeps, and bells and pips and tings. Some regular, some not, some loud, some soft. Some rhythmic, some a shock. But together, they add up to silence.

The air conditioner. The whirring of fans. The coughing. The screeching. Murmurs of pain. Laughing. Crying. Drilling. Hammering. All noise, noise, noise. Added together, they are nothing.

Nothing.

If I try. If I really try, I can pick out a single sound. Concentrate on it, then listen behind the sound. Screen it out, and beyond, there is silence.

Surreal, welcome, beautiful silence.

But then, an intrusion again. A door. A curtain. Footsteps. A phone rings. A door tings. A bed crashes. A patient shouts. An orderly runs quickly. A loud car revs its engine outside.

Noise envelops. Noise involves. Noise interferes. Noise keeps me awake, it lulls me to sleep.

Noise.

Noise.

With nothing else, noise is to be welcomed. I hear noise, there-

fore I am. But sometimes. Often. It is too much. Too loud, I can't cope. I want silence. But here, there is never silence. Not without effort.

Silence with effort.

I wonder.

I wonder if I really want the noise.

I wonder if I really want the silence.

6

Click

"Hi David." *It was Nurse Gail.*

"So, we're going to get you down for an EEG brain scan this morning. This is Charlie, he's our porter."

"Can he hear me?"

"We like to talk to our patients, Charlie, even if we don't know if they can hear us."

"Okay, hello David. I'm Charlie. I'm going to wheel you down to the scanning department. So, we'll just lift him at the shoulders here, Gail. That's it."

"Okay, David. Here we go. Off to the scan department."

"Ah, Doctor, I have your patient here." *It was Nurse Gail.*

"Shall we walk and talk, Nurse? Is that responsible adult coming this morning?" *It was Doctor Atwan. Woman's voice. Cold voice.*

"Ah, looks like this is him now."

"Hey, sorry I'm late. Couldn't find the department."

It was Dillon. Gail and Dillon. Friendly voices.

"So, what's happening?"

"We're going to be scanning David's brain today, then

offering him some stimuli. We'll measure any electronic signals - brain waves if you like. Then they'll bring out the pins again, and brushes, and a little light hammer. Just to see if we can get any brain reaction out of David."

"Will it hurt him?"

Always the caring questions.

"If he's conscious of it, it'll be pin pricks at worst. Then Doctor Atwan is going to ask some questions to see if there's any reaction."

"Right. Let's get this over with." *It was Doctor Atwan.*

"Okay, David, I'm going to start with some basic testing, to get the EEG set up correctly."

I don't know that voice. Dillon, who is it?

"Doctor, are you happy for me to proceed?"

I don't like this Dillon. I'm not comfortable. Who is that? Who just spoke? Don't let her touch me.

"Go ahead. I'll come back for a report later."

"Okay, David, I'm going to shine a light into your eyes. First left, and now right. And now left again. And now right."

The stranger again. Get her away.

"Okay, first right ear."

Click. Click.

I can't hear you. I won't hear you, stranger.

Now, left ear.

Click. Click.

Nope.

"Fine, now brush. Right cheek. Left cheek. And now right back of hand. Left back of hand. Left knee. And, oh, well left outer thigh."

Dillon, I thought you were protecting me?

"Okay, reaction hammer. Right elbow. No physical reaction. Left elbow. No physical reaction. Left knee. Okay. Left thigh."

"Needles, please."

"Thank you, and right cheek needle. Left cheek needle. Right elbow. Left elbow. And right knee. And foot - oh, sorry. Left, erm, thigh."

"And now neck, please?"

"Okay, right of neck. And left of neck."

Who is she, Dillon?

"Thank you, that completes the physical tests."

"Poor man. Is he your partner?"

Oh, she does care. I'm sorry. I was just afraid.

"No, I'm his responsible adult."

He's taking care of me.

"No-one has come forward?"

"Not yet."

"What a shame."

"Yes. What do they call you?"

"Sorry? I'm Esta."

"No, I mean your job title?"

"Oh, are you ready? I'm an electroencephalogramist or basically an EEG technician.

"Oh, I'm Dillon. Just plain Dillon."

Plain, Dillon? You saved my life!

"Pleased to meet you." *It was Esta.* "Let's hope David's family turn up soon."

Family? No Dillon. I don't have a family. No family, understand?

"Yes, I hope so."

"It's a shambles out there. Have you see the Minister? Making public statements of apology to the Saudis?"

"Sorry?"

"The government, Dillon. It's all about the money,

sucking up to the Saudis and their oil. Arms sales. Not human lives. That Saudi Prince has passed away, but David here, he's still alive. Yet, not a word." *It was Esta.*

"Well, it's not my place to say. You seem very passionate about it." *It was Dillon.*

"Yeah, sorry. Amnesty International member. Don't bring it to work, etcetera. Still, when you look at what happened. It's not like the Saudis are expressing their sympathy for everyone at the parade. And given they buy so many arms from the UK, they can twist our government whichever way they want. It's how they run Saudi Arabia, and now they're trying to do it here."

"Like I say..."

"I understand. Just a bit cross. Hey, no mention to the good doctor, eh?"

"I understand Esta."

Cross, Esta. I know cross. I know anger. I know hate.

"Anyway, sorry. David, I need to talk to Doctor Atwan now, take a look at your results as they come through. I'll be back in about an hour."

Steps.

"You did good, David."

I like being alone with you, Dillon. You give me comfort.

"Look, I've brought that Times down from the ward. We never did get to talk about the whales."

Shuffle.

"Two orcas have been spotted having a whale of a time off the Cornish coast. Experts believe this is the first sighting of the UK's only resident population of killer whales travelling this far south..."

Comforting voice. I'm sorry. I need to...

Sleep.

"Hi David, it's Esta again. Doctor Atwan and Mr Kendrick are with me too. We've got some questions for you. We're going to hope to get some of those brain neurons firing off."

Where's Dillon? Are you there?

"I'm holding your left hand right now. I'm going to squeeze it quite hard. I want you to concentrate to see if you can feel anything. Are you ready? And squeeze."

I can't feel anything Esta. Where is Dillon?

"That's great David. And squeeze again."

Still nothing.

"David, this isn't about whether you can respond. I just want you to think about my squeezing your hand. See if you can feel any connection at all. Picture me squeezing your hand."

Nothing. I feel nothing. I can't imagine what it feels like. What feeling something feels like.

"You're doing great David. Doctor?"

Silence.

"Should I?"

Dillon, you are there.

"Doctor, that might be interesting?" *It was Esta.*

"Yes, go ahead." *Cold Doctor Atwan.*

"David, I'm holding your other hand now."

I can think of that. I CAN THINK OF IT! My God, can I feel it? Or just think of it?

"Okay, I'm going to squeeze. I want you to think. Concentrate on my squeeze, okay?"

Oh please, let me feel it. Please, Dillon. I need to feel something. I can't feel you squeezing. I want to. I can think of it, but I can't feel you. I'm sorry, I want to feel something. I want to feel you.

"Doctor?" *It was Esta.*

"No, nothing on the scan."

Not nothing. Something. I want to feel. Let me feel his hand.

"Okay, David, that's good. We're going to ask you some questions." *It was Esta.*

"Do you know your real name David?"

David? No, not David. I don't remember.

"And are you from London?"

What is London? Yes, I think yes, London. South London. Green spaces.

"Do you have a baseline Doctor?"

"Yes, Esta, carry on."

"David, I want you to think of an apple. A green, juicy apple. Can you do that? Really concentrate. Green, juicy apple."

Apple. I don't know green. I don't know juicy. Apple. A is for apple. A is for angel.

"Okay, now quickly David, think of a banana. A long, yellow banana."

I don't know banana. I don't know yellow. I think I know long. Yes, long and wide and short and tall and long.

"Doctor?" *It was Esta.*

"Continue."

"David, I want you to think of something really happy. Think of something that makes you really happy. Christmas. Or a boyfriend. Or the sunshine. Really, really happy. Can you think of that?"

I don't know these words. Sunshine. Heat, warmth. Warm in bed. Warm, burn. Feet, burn. No, be happy. I know happy, I'm sure I do. I don't have a boyfriend. Never. My feet feel hot.

"Okay, quickly David, let's think of something sad. Something angry."

Angry. I want to talk. Let me talk. Angry. No pain, but lots of angry. Bomb makes me angry. Hospital, makes me angry. Hate, makes me angry.

"That's fine, thank you. Now, let's think of cold. Can you remember being cold."

Tired. I don't know cold.

"And now David, can you think of being very hot?"

Holiday, hot. Bomb, hot. Fire, hot. No, angry hot. Water. I'm so tired. Please, let me stop.

"You're doing great. Now I think we have some questions from your responsible adult, now?"

I don't know these words.

"David, it's Dillon. Do you remember me? Do you know me? Do you recognise my voice?"

"Mr Kendrick, you need one question at a time, I think." *It was Doctor Atwan.*

"Yes, Doctor, I'm sorry."

"David, it's Dillon. Do you know me?"

Yes, yes. You are kind to me. You saved my life.

"David, can you remember your family. Father, mother?"

No. No father. Please, no father. Mum, poor Mum. No, Mum. They hate me. No family.

"You're doing well, David." *It was Esta.*

"David, do you miss anyone? Is there someone special you miss?"

No special. Never special. I am not special.

"I think we've seen enough." *It was Doctor Atwan.*

Thank you, Sophie.

Yes, I'm outside 10 Downing Street, hearing interesting revelations today that the Saudi Embassy has announced it is cutting off contact with the British government until the

Metropolitan Police reveal the results of their current investigation into the London Pride bombings.

This is very likely to cause a political crisis between the two nations.

My understanding is that Foreign Secretary Dominic Hall has appealed to the Saudi royal family directly for talks, but has so far been rebuffed. If ties are completely severed, business leaders fear lucrative contracts between Saudi Arabia and Great Britain could be at stake, risking thousands of British jobs.

Prince Yusuf Al-Ghamdi, who was said to be shopping close to Piccadilly Circus when the explosion took place, was killed in the bombings in London on 21st June.

Before the Embassy closed contact with the British government, the Ambassador outlined two demands: a thorough explanation of why Saudi citizens had been put at risk in London, and a guarantee that the perpetrators of the attack be brought to justice. Commentators are now speculating that the Saudis may soon ban travel visas to the country for British citizens.

Commentators have noted that Saudi Arabia does not have an independent judiciary system, and may be demanding something the crisis...

Door.

"David?"

Click.

"Sorry. It's me, Dillon. How you getting on today?"

Sad.

"I think the doctor will be along soon."

Knock.

Door.

"Good morning Mr Kendrick. Nurse."

"Good morning Doctor."

"Okay, so I had my joint clinical conference with my colleagues yesterday afternoon, after David's EEG scans. We invited in an expert in locked-in syndrome, who was kind enough to join us online from York University Hospital. He has been following David's case."

"I see." *It was Dillon.*

"I have to say that things aren't looking good for him, or for any recovery."

"For David."

"I'm sorry?" *It was Doctor Atwan.*

"I don't want to speak out of turn, Doctor, but I think we all should call him David. He's not just a 'he'. David is a person. What I mean is, David may not be conscious, but he's still here."

"If it means that much to you, Mr Kendrick." *It was Doctor Atwan.*

"I think it would mean a lot to David."

Oh, Dillon.

"Well, David, Mr Kendrick, we concluded in clinic yesterday that he - sorry David - has no sensations whatsoever in relation to his physical or mental state. No brain function, no reactions whatsoever to stimuli. He can't hear, he can't feel, he can't see. There is no brain reaction whatsoever. In conclusion, the patient is brain dead. Mr Kendrick, you can call him David all you like, but this patient is in a permanent vegetative state which, in our judgement, he will not recover from."

"Oh."

"Oh, indeed. In fact, if the brain continues its disfunction in this manner, there is very likely to be a slow decline in his condition. He'll start struggling to breathe. Perhaps stop creating the blood cells he needs. He could have a heart attack at any point. We've already seen that. Mr Kendrick,

David will wither away or he'll have a stroke or angina seizure. He could die any time, or he could lie here for years.

"Call him what you like, Mr Kendrick. He is not conscious of himself or his existence. He cannot hear me. We will continue to treat him until his parents or another next of kin comes forward, and then we'll advise them that we'd like to allow him to die. If they agree, we will remove sustenance for his own benefit."

"Thank you, Doctor, whatever is best for David."

"I'm sorry, Dillon." *It was Nurse Gail.*

"You are David's responsible adult. That is your right and responsibility. Until someone comes to claim him. But I'm afraid the result is inevitable." *It was the doctor.*

Silence.

Dillon? It's okay Dillon.

"I understand. Thanks."

"Okay, all done here. Nurse?"

"I'll follow you out in a moment."

Door.

Click.

"You okay, Mr Kendrick? I'm very sorry."

"Of course. You know, I'm not allowed to get emotionally involved."

Wait, do you care for me, Dillon? I'm not gay. Are you? Please don't be gay. I want to be your friend. You don't understand.

"I'm sorry about the doctor, she's very frank. She's seen a lot. If it's any consolation, David died on that Pride day. This isn't David. David was there, marching for his rights. Proud to be who he was. We should all be proud of him."

"I understand. Such a shame."

Wait, Dillon. I don't care if you're gay. Stay with me. Please don't give up on me.

"What about next of kin?"

"Mr Kendrick, it's time for the medical process to take its course. Without a next of kin, or someone to name him, it is convention for him to be allowed to die. And if I was his parent, I'm not sure I'd disagree."

"Sure. Of course, you're right. When will the press know?" *It was Dillon.*

"This place leaks like a bucket, Mr Kendrick."

"Yes, I suppose so. It feels like giving up."

"Mr Kendrick, it's more like letting go."

"I understand. Letting go."

NO! NO! I am here. I AM here!

7

Breaking news this hour, as new footage posted on social media channel YouTube appears to show a figure carrying a green rucksack moments before the bomb went off at the London Pride bombing on 21st June.

Police have previously stated they were looking for evidence of a green rucksack at the parade, and had identified it as the possible source of the bomb. Our special correspondent Dean Joyce reports from New Scotland Yard.

That's right, Sophie. This is quite a revelation today, and we have chosen not to show the YouTube video for fear of causing distress.

However, I'm able to report that the person carrying the rucksack which the police say they were looking for, is wearing what might be described as full traditional Islamic dress.

He or she is seen on the video walking close to the Black Lives Matter banner. The image pans away from the figure and across the crowd, before a loud explosion is heard. It is then that the footage rapidly ends.

Police say they are investigating the footage closely, and are reminding the public not to speculate as to the identity of the person.

They say they are working hard to verify the YouTube video, who posted it, and whether it may have been doctored.

When I looked this morning, Sophie, the video had already received twenty five thousand views.

My understanding is that YouTube has refused requests to take it down, stating that it does not show graphic violence, and may help investigations into the bombing. A number of news websites are also carrying the video.

Police say they will use the new footage to open up avenues of investigation, and are again appealing for any witnesses prompted by the footage to examine their own photographs and videos of the scene. Back to you, Sophie, in the studio.

Thank you, Dean. Can I confirm speculation that the bombing was carried out by a man is cast into doubt by the footage?

Well, Sophie, I can only repeat that the police have asked the public not to speculate. But I can report that commentators on social media have suggested the person carrying the rucksack in its left hand had a female figure, rather than a man's, and that he or she was particularly short.

Some are comparing the figure's apparent height to a window ledge close by, concluding the person carrying the rucksack was no more than five and a half feet tall.

Once again, this is all speculation, and we await further confirmation by the police.

Knock.

Door

"Hello! It's Sheila, come to change your sheets."

Door.

"Ah, Marjorie, come in. Good to see you. I'm already started. Okay, lovely David, we're just going to lift you up."

"Heard the news, Sheila?"

"Can't avoid it."

"I knew it. I just knew it. Don't know why the police didn't see it coming."

"Well, you did say. We'll just lift up your bum there David. They say it was a girl, Marjorie. The Burka Bomber, for God's sake. According to my paper anyway. Not sure why they let anyone covering their face anywhere near that parade."

"Makes you shiver. Not sure any of us is safe anywhere any more. And men could disguise themselves in Burkas."

"No, this was definitely a girl. The size of her, on the video. Tiny, she was."

"Word is she was white?"

"You're joking, Marj?"

"Yeah, a white Muslim convert. They're the worst, aren't they? I mean, extremists. Not ordinary Muslims. And definitely, not. Well, not good ethnic people like you Marj. Most Muslims, they're lovely. Their music and everything. And food."

"Yeah, it's the extremists."

"The internet they say. Okay, David, what do we think, sitting up today?"

"Yeah, sitting up, Sheila. Give him some dignity. You got that nappy changed."

"Poor man."

"Poor everyone at that parade."

"Okay, I'll get the flowers changed in here. They're looking a bit sullen."

"Leave the TV on for you David?"

"Word is he can't hear? Doesn't even know he's alive. Like a bug or something."

"Well, I can't stand the silence for him. Doesn't feel right."

"I suppose you're right, Sheila."

Click.

"See you tomorrow, David."

"Bye, David."

8

"Hi David, come in Brendan."

Brendan? Who's Brendan? Dillon, why have you been away so long?

"Nurse Gail, this is Brendan."

"Is it you? Is it?"

I don't know that voice. Who is it, Dillon? Who have you brought to see me? I don't want him here.

"David, this is Brendan. He thinks he might know you? I hope you don't mind, I've given him permission to come and see you. Is that okay with you, Nurse? He doesn't want to go via the police because, well, maybe he'll explain."

"Are you sure, Dillon?" *It was Nurse Gail.*

No, take him away.

"Hi David. I'm sorry, I'm not sure. We might have met at The Windmill? Well, in the alleyway behind actually. But it was dark. I'm so sorry about what happened to you."

"Do you think you know him?"

"Not by name. He looks familiar but, well, it was a one night thing. One evening, actually. You know, outside the pub. If I can just..."

"No, no you can't."

Click. Click.

What? What's happening, Dillon?

"Oops. It's okay, I can get a better look at him this way."

"Give me that phone. Gail, call security."

What? What's wrong?

"I didn't give you permission to photograph him."

"And who are you?"

"I'm his responsible adult. I get to make decisions about him. You have to delete that photo right now. Gail, can you call security?"

"Okay. Sorry, here we go. Oh, oops. I just sent it."

"Oh, you bastard."

"Sorry, no. No, I don't think I do know David. My mistake."

"Give me that fucking phone."

"Mmm, don't think so. Goodbye folks."

Door.

"Ah shit. What have I done?"

"Hello, security? Please stop a man at the entrance. Tight jeans, T-shirt. *Hope for David* written on it. Get his phone."

"Doesn't matter, Gail."

"What?"

"If he's texted that picture, it's out."

"Oh."

Silence.

"Shit. I'm so sorry David. I'm supposed to be protecting you. I wqas just trying to help get you identified. Give you a name. What a mess up. Sorry, Nurse, how do I register this. Is there some security procedure?"

You are protecting me, Dillon. You're all I have, right now. I'm pleased you didn't know him. What's wrong with my photograph anyway? Do I look bad?

"It wasn't your fault, Mr Kendrick. That guy will be after big bucks for that photo."

"He was probably some sleaze bag tabloid journalist."

"Yeah, like I say, not your fault."

I don't care, Dillon. You are both my guardian angels. It's not going to get any worse is it? Just don't go. It doesn't matter. Just please don't go.

Door.

"So, what the hell happened here? DI Ling, turn off that bloody TV. Let's have a look. It's pretty much an exact match. How the hell did someone get in here to get that photo?"

"I'm not sure, he's supposed to be protected."

"Where's his protection then? Where's that guy who is supposed to be his responsible adult. He's messed up big time. It could interfere with our investigation."

Door.

"Oh, Detective Chief Inspector Pierce. DI Ling." *It was Dillon.*

"Ah, Mr Kendrick. May I ask, politely, what the fuck happened? DI Ling, pass him the newspaper please."

"I've seen it."

"So, you saw the shit has hit the fan and landed all over my team, Mr Kendrick. Do you know what pressure I'm under from the Home Secretary? We've found the bomber, we need to clear up the case."

"Mr Kendrick, we are having to examine how this photo came about, and how it became plastered across every newspaper and TV station across the UK." *It was DI Ling.*

"You are supposed to be responsible for David until any

next of kin comes forward, or until the courts take over, am I right?" *It was DCI Pierce.*

"Yes, I failed. I've reported it. I thought I'd found someone who could identify him. Someone from the vigil outside."

There's a vigil still? For me?

"So, what, you invited them up?"

"He thought he might have had, well, an encounter with David the night before the attack."

An encounter?

"And you believed him?" *It was DI Ling.*

"I didn't realise."

"That's very naive, Mr Kendrick. The press are biting their arms off to get more on this story. And you've just gifted them a bloody photograph of David looking like this."

Looking like what, Dillon? What's wrong with me? Am I disgusting to you?

"Now, I need to take a statement about this man who took the picture, but to be honest what he has done isn't a crime. Because you invited him in. Jesus. Who trains these responsible adults?"

"It was my fault. Completely. And I've reported myself to Westminster social services. I'm waiting for a response. In the meantime, I'm staying with David."

"What?"

"Until asked to stand down, he has a right to my representation?"

"Okay, whatever. Have there been any signs of consciousness? Any movements?"

"Nothing to report, officer. Have you spoken to the doctors about his condition?"

"Not yet, Mr Kendrick. We've been trying to pin down this bomber. Kinda busy, you know. Pressure from the government. The Home Office is on my back. The Saudis want my blood. Really could have done with not having this on our plate too. We need to clean up this mess, quickly."

"Like I say."

"Yes, yes, you're sorry."

"Well, it's essential that you or the doctors let us know the moment he's communicating." *It was DI Ling.*

"I'm not sure that's going to happen, officer."

"Sorry?"

"You'll need to talk to the doctors, I think. But if anything changes under my watch, you'll be the first to know."

"Your watch? Well, that'll be something." *It was DCI Pierce.*

"Can I ask, has there been any contact from next of kin yet? Anyone at all?" *It was Dillon.*

"No, Mr Kendrick. The helpline has run dry. But maybe your new super photo shoot will generate some interest. I've got to go out there now and make a statement. We'll have to separate the crazies out. Thanks for that job, by the way."

"What else can I say?"

"Sir, you are responsible adult for David. You have nothing to do with this investigation, so keep your nose out. Otherwise I shall have you removed."

"Yes, DCI Pierce."

"Good, then. Okay, DI Ling, who else is on our list?"

Door.

"I'm sorry David, I've messed this up so badly. Let's hope a family member comes forward soon. You need someone else."

I don't want anyone else. I don't have a family.

"Sorry, David. I'll see you later."

Wake.

Wait, what is that?

Maybe I'm still asleep. Or maybe it woke me up.

Like a whining, only not. A thumping. Rhythmic. It's different. Different from what I've been hearing.

Thump, thump, thump.

Whistling too, or crying out?

Or maybe my imagination. I don't remember sounds. I can't picture them, join them up with what I see. What I used to see.

Thump, thump, thump. Whine, whine, whine.

It's, is it music? Is that what music sounds like?

Only it's so distant.

Thump, whoo, thump, whoo, thump, whoo.

And now different.

Bang, ba-bada-ba-ba, bang, ba-bada-ba-ba.

It's fun. Getting closer.

Whistles.

Bang, ba-bada-ba-ba, bang, ba-bada-ba-ba. Beep, beep, beep.

Bang, ba-bada-ba-ba, bang, ba-bada-ba-ba. Beep, beep, beep.

Wait.

No.

God, no!

It's not Pride. Please, tell me it's not Pride.

Bang, ba-bada-ba-ba, bang, ba-bada-ba-ba. Beep, beep, beep.

Bang, ba-bada-ba-ba, bang, ba-bada-ba-ba. Beep, beep, beep.

No! Stop! The explosion is coming. It's too late. It's too late. Scatter. Stop the drums. Get away. Get somewhere safe.

Ba-bada-ba-ba, ba-bad a-ba-ba, ba-bada-ba-ba, ba-bad a-ba-ba, beep, beep, beep, BEEP!

A countdown. Oh fuck. Close your eyes. It's coming. Any second now.

Ba-ba-ba-ba-ba-ba-ba...

Oh God.

Swish. Click.

Silence.

Wait. It's the door.

Ba-ba-ba-ba-ba-ba-ba...

"Oh David, David!" *It was Nurse Gail.*

"I wish you could hear them. They've come all the way from Soho. Here, let me open the window."

Crunch.

Bang, ba-bada-ba-ba, bang, ba-bada-ba-ba. Beep, beep, beep.

Louder now.

"I can see them David, right below. They've stopped the traffic. Underneath your window. Should I wave? It's only two floors down."

What's going on, Nurse?

"Oh, I'd feel silly. They might not even see me. Go on, I'll give them a wave."

Silence.

Cheering. Whistling. Ba-ba-ba-ba.

"Justice for David. Justice for queers. Justice for David. Justice for queers. Justice for David. Justice for queers."

"Oh, dear, David. I think I set that off. Sorry! Here let me close the window."

Quieter now.

"You're their hero, David. You're my hero too. Oops, shouldn't say that. But you're a brave man. I'm so sorry this happened to you all."

What? I don't understand. What did I do? They don't know

me. No-one knows me. Tell them to go, Gail. Tell them to take it all away.

"David, it's hard to say, stupid really, but I'm really proud of you. For keeping up the fight, you know? For your rights. Hope I'm not getting carried away, but this could be a moment of transformation for your community. Another Stonewall, my sister says. I don't know. People will remember you for the rest of history."

In the distance now.

Bang, ba-bada-ba-ba, bang, ba-bada-ba-ba. Beep, beep, beep.

Bang, ba-bada-ba-ba, bang, ba-bada-ba-ba.

Until I can't hear it any longer.

9

Door.

"Quick, Marj, we need to get the news on. David, hope you don't mind? It's about the bombing."

Click.

"Should we sit on the bed, Sheila?"

This morning new information has been released about the fatal bombing at London's Pride Festival three weeks ago. Police have now officially named the suspected bomber as fifteen year old Noor Hisham, a convert to Islam, previously known as Charlotte Brookes from Wimbledon, South West London.

Our correspondant Dean Joyce reports.

Thank you, Sophie.

Yes, it is understood the bomber, wearing a full Islamic burka on the day of Pride - that's a long black dress and head-scarf - with a rainbow garland around her neck, was carrying a rucksack in her hands. It is now strongly suspected to have contained a home-made incendiary device.

CCTV obtained by The Sun newspaper shows a figure in

black clothing carrying the rucksack close to the Black Lives Matter banner at the Pride parade, moments before the explosion took place.

I'm outside Scotland Yard now, where police said in a press conference this morning that they suspect the bomber acted alone, though are investigating the circumstances leading up to the event.

They say Noor Hisham could not have put together the bomb without some specialist training. However, our own investigations at Express News this morning found multiple sites on the internet where information is freely available about creating a device.

Police have taken away all computers and electronics from the Brookes' family home for further investigation.

Meantime, protests have been taking place outside mosques across the UK, while debate about the bombing and policing of the event remains in contention. There is also a vigil outside of St Michael's hospital, where one victim, known as David, lies in a coma.

Thank you Dean Joyce.

"Oh, my goodness. It *was* a girl, Marj. I can't believe it."

"How sad. I mean, the whole thing."

"Sad for David. You won't get any sympathy from me for that bomber girl. God knows what the parents were thinking. A white girl too. Fifteen, did they say? All she needed was some good parental influence. Dereliction of duty if you ask me."

"Shocking. This whole thing is shocking. Better get David sorted, anyway. It's so sad."

"Converted, they said."

"Sheila, I don't want to talk about this any more. Muslim

or not, that don't matter to me. Still a young girl. All those deaths."

"Well, excuse me."

"Let's just be quiet, eh? Give David a break from all this chatter?"

"Sure. Whatever."

Silence.

And now we turn to the political implications of this morning's revelations about the bomb, and our political editor Natasha Harding, who I understand is back to her usual spot outside Parliament.

That's right Sophie. I'm here outside of the House of Commons, where Home Secretary Francis Gardiner is due to make a statement later today.

Early indications are that he will say this was a single incident, and that the public should not fear for their safety. The real threat, he will say, is the internet and its potential to corrupt a generation of young people. He will call on social media companies to do more to ban extremist material.

He will also call for calm among the public, and ask for comments and speculations on social media about the bombing to be balanced.

However, it is becoming more clear that the government is facing a foreign relations crisis, with regards to Saudi Arabia.

You will remember, Sophie, that the British and Saudi governments have long been strategic partners, and Saudi Arabia is seen as Britain's biggest friend in the Middle East.

My understanding is that Foreign Secretary Dominic Hall is under pressure, as accusations from Riyadh are that the

Metropolitan Police have been slow in investigations into the bombing.

A member of the family was killed and some of his aides were injured on the day. Our understanding is that the Foreign Secretary will fly out to Saudi Arabia in the next few days for emergency talks with the Supreme Leader...

10

Knock.

Door.

"Come in Judge Millar, this is David."

"Thank you Doctor Atwan. I see. May I take a seat."

"Of course."

"Sir, you've already met Mr Kendrick. He's been looking after David."

"Well, Mr Kendrick, for the record I want to reiterate our appreciation of your service to the community and the judicial system. You're giving people like David here a voice they wouldn't otherwise have. I hope everyone has been behaving themselves?"

"David, our hospital management asked us to bring Judge Millar down to meet you. Can you confirm that's okay, Mr Kendrick?"

"Yes, of course." *It was Dillon.*

It must be something really important today.

"Doctor, can you please restate the current medical situation with David?" *It was the judge.*

"Judge, my understanding is that David is in a permanent vegetative state. He has no feeling, hearing or senses whatsoever, and our understanding is that it is very unlikely he has any sense of being alive at all. We don't use the term any more, but in old speak, David is brain dead."

I'm in here, Doctor.

"I understand the terms, Doctor, please continue."

"Thank you Judge. We have run numerous tests with David, with Mr Kendrick present throughout, and have not been able to elicit any responses from him. There is no significant brain activity, and none in response to any stimuli we've offered. We have the paperwork ready for you to take away. Our diagnosis is cerebromedullospinal disconnection, resulting in total form pseudocoma. Total Locked In syndrome, Sir."

"Doctor, what is your prognosis for this individual?"

"Judge, he will not recover from this state. It is also my opinion that if his brain is not further stimulated, it is likely to lose function. That could lead to seizures, negative effects on the unconscious brain functions, and ultimately death."

"Be clearer, Doctor Atwan, for the sake of Mr Kendrick please?"

"Of course. If his brain starts to wither away, the natural brain functions we all have - breathing, organs, heart function - may be affected negatively. He could have a heart attack, or kidney failure. David has already had three cardiac arrests.

"Judge, he has no next of kin, so it falls to the hospital to decide upon the next move for David. Our recommendation will be to cease sustenance, and allow David to pass away. We believe this is the most humane way to proceed and, also in terms of resources most efficient."

"Efficient?" *It was Dillon.*

Checking for me. Always caring for me.

"Mr Kendrick, I've been advised by my seniors that David is taking up an undue amount of our resources. A bed. Emergency equipment. Staffing. Medication. I'm afraid, they believe that keeping David alive could actually be risking the lives of others who have more chance of recovery. The legislation requires us to consider hospital resources in this kind of decision."

"Has the Secretary of State been consulted in David's case?"

"Judge Millar, the Secretary of State for Health is aware of the case. She has advised us to take the lead, with your legal advice."

"I see. Do we envisage any resistance to your proposal?"

"Religious groups, perhaps, your honour. But given the contradictions in these circumstances, the board has advised me it might be muted."

"Can you explain, again, please, Doctor?"

"Sorry, Judge. David was injured at the London Pride Festival, and our assumption is that he is gay, or at very least was marching in support of gay rights. The kinds of groups that might object to our proposal are also those likely to condemn homosexuality as a sin. Some, I suspect, would not like to expose themselves to such a contradiction."

"I understand that, though I would advise that you certainly consider any petition that is offered, from whatever party. That is their right, though as you know the hospital will make the final decision."

"Of course, Judge."

Silence.

"Okay, this is what I'm going to do. I'll ask you to file your recommendations to me by the end of the month. Mr Kendrick, can you ask if Westminster social services have their own opinion, or would defer to the hospital? I'll have my office write to the Director there anyway."

"If other interested groups would like to petition you, then you have the statutory obligation listen to them. Though I'm not going to go searching for them. And of course, if any next of kin turn up, that resets everything.

"My understanding of the law is that David here must be in a consistent vegetative state for at least six months, before Canh can be removed."

"Canh, Sir?" *It was Dillon.*

"Judge, if I may? Clinically assisted nutrition and hydration. It means we're feeding him nutrients through a tube to keep him alive." *It was Doctor Atwan.*

"My advice will take into account exactly *how* David is being fed when the time comes, Doctor Atwan. Please do not forget that."

"Understood, Sir."

"Mr Kendrick, this will be set out in my eventual recommendation, but the law states that Canh can be removed if there is no realistic short term chance of recovery. If there are no objections, and a full six months have passed, the hospital will have my legal advice to proceed given no change in circumstances." *It was the judge.*

"There wouldn't be any objections, surely? Wouldn't it be the kindest thing to do, to let him go?" *It was Dillon.*

"I'm sorry, Mr Kendrick, but these things have been tried and tested in court, and a precedent has been set. It is a controversial issue. Some would argue that removal of Canh is assisted killing. Others, that removal of Canh is only allowing the original cause of death to continue. It's actually very complex, which is why the hospital management asked me to come in."

"Can you clarify, what are the circumstances in which

we might not be able to proceed with withdrawal?" *It was the doctor.*

"Well, if David's family appear and object. The Home Office also may wish to take a different view, should that happen or if circumstances change. I'll set an initial consideration date of one month's time. You'll receive a legal advice letter from me after that time. Any more questions?"

I have questions.

Silence.

"Thank you judge." *It was Doctor Atwan.*

Door.

"I'll stay for a while." *It was Dillon.*

Silence.

Dillon? Are you still there?

"Oh David. David, David, David. I'm so sorry this has happened to you."

I'm sorry too, Dillon. I don't want to be taken away from you. Are you close, Dillon?

"I'm holding your hand, David, I hope you don't mind. Just in case you can hear me. I know I'm not supposed to get emotionally involved. But, well, anyway. I've never lost anyone before."

You haven't lost me, Dillon. I'm right here.

"I don't know how to react. I did the training and everything, but I didn't expect this."

I'm here for you Dillon.

"I guess I need to report this. The department is all set up to help us unload. Just, this feels a bit different. Like I'm losing a brother or something."

A brother?

"Well, I guess we have a couple more months. That's for the best, I'm sure. We can get used to the idea."

Silence.

"Ah, for fuck's sake. This is ridiculous. You can't hear me. You can't feel my hand. What am I doing here? Okay, right, this is silly. I don't even know you."

Don't say that Dillon. Don't say that. Don't go.

Door.

Silence.

Dillon?

Dillon, are you there?

Please, don't leave me alone. I want to be with you Dillon. Oh God, I'm so scared of dying alone.

Welcome to the Sunshine Sofa this morning, and thank you Sophie Horgan for the news.

Quite a revelation yesterday, Isha?

It's quite unbelievable, isn't it Ed? The London Pride bomb was the work of a fifteen year old Muslim convert from Wimbledon. It's really quite the story. Shall we do our Morning Media Roundup?

Yes, Isha. So, the press are having a field day, of course. Let's take a quick look at the morning papers. Here, we have The Sun newspaper claiming credit for identifying the bomber, with the release of footage of the young woman as she was marching with the Black Lives Matter protest.

An editorial in that paper says that the pictures gave the Metropolitan Police the extra leg up it desperately needed to pin down the identity of the bomber. Isha?

That's right, and The Times newspaper also implies the Met police have been caught on the hoof. They too say it was only social media that helped to identify the suspect. The Times also carries a photo of Noor Hisham in front of the Black Lives Matter banner, carrying the now infamous green rucksack. And it really is that green rucksack that's been the crux of all of this. I even checked my own closet for one, did you?

Do you know what, Isha, I did! And my kid's cupboards. You forget what you've got, don't you. But I think everyone wanted to help the police on this, I guess checking our own stuff gives us a sense of solidarity.

So, the press have also been focussing again on this photo of the sole remaining survivor of the bomb. It's pretty difficult to look at.

That's right, Ed. I'm not sure how the press got that picture of David - as St Michael's hospital have named him. He remains in a critical condition, according to The Times, in what is called a permanent vegetative state.

He has no sight, no sense of hearing, or touch, and unlikely any brain function. The Time's sources say the man is very unlikely to survive. I have to say, there has been a huge sympathy for David, hasn't there?

Yes, I don't think we've seen such a gathering of feeling among the general public for a critically injured patient in this way for a long time.

Isha, perhaps you're a little young, but I remember the Hillsborough football stadium disaster of 1989. It was a real moment for the UK, probably because it affected football which remains real uniting language, I guess.

Well, maybe the LGBTQ plus community are getting their own sympathy moment just now? I mean, Isha, I've been over to St Michael's myself. Laid some flowers, among many thousands of others. There's a 24 hour vigil, candles, singing. It's quite lovely to see.

Yes, I've passed the vigil. So, if we turn now to the Daily Mail, Ed, we have the headline: 340 years. That, claims the paper, is the number of years that Noor Hisham would have faced in prison if convicted of the bombing, had she not been killed by her own device.

Wait, Isha, would she have been old enough to stand trial? I guess we'll never know.

The Mail also features reports from Noor Hisham's school. Unnamed sources say the young woman had become removed from her friends, disappeared for long periods of time, and had left most of her online friendship groups. A Mail editorial also claims there is evidence that Noor Hisham attended meetings of both the London Black Lives Matter Congress last year and the LGBTQ plus Muslim Support group. The editorial says she was likely to be gathering intelligence.

Meanwhile, we have a softer approach from The Guardian newspaper, Ed. They carry a short interview with Noor Hisham's father, Peter Brookes. He told the paper that his daughter Emily Brookes had recently converted Islam and he asked for calm.

She had, and I quote Mr Brookes here, 'been a difficult teenager.' But Mr Brookes told the Guardian he refused to believe the young woman was capable of the bombing. He asked for the family to be given space to grieve their daughter, as well as all the other victims of the bombing. He appealed to the police to double check their investigations, and said he pleaded with social media companies to look out for false accusations.

Unfortunately, it doesn't look like that request has been heeded, Ed?

Well, in The Telegraph, Mr Brookes has been challenged in particular for, again it's a quote from the editorial, 'questionable parenting'. 'Any father who allows his so-called clever, untarnished daughter to be converted by extremists, certainly cannot claim to be a good parent in any sense that a right-minded person would understand it.'

And, I have to say, Isha, that appears to be the general gist of comments on social media right now. Very little sympathy for Noor Hisham's father for refusing to accept his daughter's guilt.

Well, suffice to say, there's going to be a lot more on this story to come. Now, over to our science team for news of a documentary series that starts tonight, Gazing at the Moon. Alistair's here to tell us more.

11

Sleep.

Silence.

When a man loves a man, who is not their brother or their father or their son, Jesus Christ calls them a sinner.

Amen.

When a man lies down with a man, Jesus Christ calls them a sinner.

Amen.

When the unfaithful men of Sodom and Gomorrah laid down with men, with beasts, the Lord our God punished them rightly with fire and hell.

Amen.

The sinful must ask for forgiveness.

Amen.

The sinful must turn again.

Amen.

The sinful must be pure in thought and deed, or else face eternal damnation of pain, and fire, and darkness.

Amen.

Let us hold these truths as immutable. Let us praise God for these truths.

Amen. Praise Lord God.

Let us praise Jesus Christ, our Saviour, who died on the cross for all of our sins.

Amen. Praise Jesus Christ.

And let those who sin and do not seek forgiveness from Jesus Christ face eternal punishment.

Amen.

These men here, before us. Let God have mercy on their souls.

Amen.

Brother Mark, do you repent of your sinful thoughts and actions.

Father forgive me. I am with sin. I beg of Your forgiveness, in the name of Your Son, Jesus Christ.

Amen.

Brother Unan, do you repent of your sinful thoughts and actions.

Father forgive me. I am with sin. I beg of Your forgiveness, in the name of Your Son, Jesus Christ.

Amen.

Brother Adam, do you repent of your sinful thoughts and actions.

Father forgive me. I am with sin. I beg of Your forgiveness, in the name of Your Son, Jesus Christ.

Amen.

Lord God, almighty Father, we ask You to forgive these young boys for their mortal sin, their crimes against You and Your one and only Son.

Together, we will work in Your service to change these boys. We will ensure they will never again sin against You, for which Jesus Christ died on the cross for all of our sins and misdemeanours. So help us, dear Lord.

Amen.

Lord, help us as we train these young men to be better. To be the loyal husbands of their wives. To father many children in Your name. To instruct their family in the way in which You, the Lord God, have determined.

Amen.

Thank you Lord God, and Jesus Christ Your only Son, for Your answer to our prayers. A sin against You from one of our community, is a sin from all of our community. Lord, we exist to serve You. Please, take us under Your watchful gaze, and support us to rebuild the purity that these young men were born with in Your name. Help us to make them sinless once more.

Amen.

Now, together. Our Father, who art in heaven, hallowed be thy name, thy kingdom come...

12

England's LGBTQ plus community, as well as religious figures, have been speaking out on the case of David, the one remaining survivor of the Pride Festival bombings. Our legal correspondent Hamish Lee reports.

Thank you, Sophie.

Doctors have concluded that the unidentified man, aged between 25 and 30, is in a vegetative state from which he will not recover. They say he has no sensations and no brain functions. However, members of the gay community are calling for a longer wait for the man to show some sentience.

At the same time, some Christian leaders are also arguing that David has a right to life, in whatever state of being he remains.

The case is complex, with legal experts and medical professionals arguing David's quality of life is so low as to be nonexistent, and that allowing him to pass away is the kindest way to proceed.

Initial legal proceedings are due in the next few days, but experts say it is likely to be weeks before any discussions take place.

> *We understand that any next of kin is yet to come forward, who under English law have a right to decide on the future of the man, though their decision could also be challenged by medics. Church leaders have already vowed to follow the case closely.*
>
> *Back to the studio, Sophie.*

Click.

"Jesus, they still leaving that TV on, David?"

Yeah. Every day. I don't mind. I like to keep up with news about myself.

"Honestly, it's like you're a superstar. Only, a really really sad case. Like, I don't know, Amy Winehouse or…"

Freddie Mercury.

"…Freddie Mercury, or that guy from the Buzzcocks."

Pete Shelley.

"Or, I don't know, David Bowie."

Keep talking. I love it when you talk to me.

"Well, David. I'm wondering if our time together is coming to an end. You see, the courts are going to take over now. I can't speak as your advocate. I don't even know what you would want. Or if you're capable of wanting anything."

I want to live. I want you to keep visiting me.

"So, I guess it's going to be the medics and the legals that decide. Whatever happens, I hope it's peaceful. There's a whole lot of fuss going on out there about you, but I hope it'll be pretty straightforward once they get down to it.

"Anyway, there's going to be a vigil outside the court when they start proceedings. Just one of respect, I think. The police have warned the protesters to keep clear."

My dad did this to me, Dillon. I wish you could hear that. I'm glad he's not found me. He's getting what he wanted. I wish I could tell you, Dillon. I wish you knew that one thing. He's the one. He's the one that did this.

All of this.

13

Knock.

Door.

"Let me see. Let me see. Oh my goodness, Adam, is it you? Is it really you?"

"Please stand back, Mrs Pound." *It was DCI Pierce.*

"He's our son. It's you, Adam? Oh my God, what did they do to you?"

Who is this? Hello? Where's Dillon? I don't know these voices. DCI Pierce, I don't know these people.

"Valerie, Lord's name please!"

Lord's name? Oh no, it can't be.

"Sorry Geoff. Adam, good grief. Can I touch him, oh my boy, my wonderful wonderful boy. The tube in his mouth, oh I can't stand it."

"Just that picture again, Mr Pound, please."

"Here. Here it is. Now, let me see my son."

"Please hold on, Mr Pound. I need to get some verification here."

Crunching.

"DCI Pierce here. Can you get me a verification on Pound, Geoff. Family members, Valerie and - Adam?"

Crunch.

Crunch.

"Postcode, please? Address?"

"15 Clifford Road, Tooting Broadway, SW14 5LA?"

Wait. No, no, no.

"Did you get that officer?"

Feedback.

Knock.

Door.

"Officer. Can we make this short? Oh, hello."

"Nurse, thanks for coming along. We're waiting for some positive identification, but we have reason to believe this couple, Mr and Mrs Pound, are the parents of David here."

"The diamond. The diamond, tell them Geoff. The diamond."

"Calm down, Valerie. And it's Adam. His name is Adam."

"Oh, please. We need to remove the tube in his mouth. Is it hurting him? I can't bear it."

"I'm sorry, Mrs Pound. What do you mean by diamond?" *It was DCI Pierce.*

"Four moles on his back. Right hand side. They make a diamond. Like stars make shapes."

"A constellation they call it, Valerie. Con-stell-a-tion. In a diamond shape."

"Nurse?"

"It's not something I've noticed. I'll call an orderly and we'll get him lifted."

"Nonsense. I can lift my own son."

"Sir, I'm going to have to ask you to take a step back." *It was DCI Pierce.*

"He's my boy, you take a step back."

"Nurse, can you call an orderly, please. Quickly?"

Door.

"Mr Pound, I'm very sorry, but this will have to be witnessed and until we have positively identified our patient here as your son, he is under the ward of the Metropolitan Police and Westminster local authority."

"Away with your junk speak. I know my son."

No. Don't touch me. You don't know me. I don't want to know you. Where is Dillon?

"Mr Pound, please step back."

"Look, look, officer. There, see..."

"Oh, my darling. It is you Adam!"

Sobbing.

"Oh my gosh, oh my gosh. Thank you Jesus." *It was Mum.*

"Plain and simple to see, officer or whatever you are. A diamond of moles. Satisfied?"

It was Dad.

Door.

"Ah, Nurse, thank you and Charlie." *It was DCI Pierce.*

"Charlie, if we can just get him lifted. Was it the right hand side?" *It was Nurse Gail.*

"That's okay. Mr Pound just identified David. I'm making a note, 10.34 a.m Mr Geoff Pound and Mrs Valerie Pound offer initial positive identity of patient known to this hospital as David."

"Adam. His name is Adam." *It was Dad. Oh my God, he's found me.*

"Adam Pound, presumably your son madam?"

"Yes, officer. His friends call him Ad."

"His age please?"

"Twenty-four." *It was Dad.*

Shuffling. Shuffle, drag. Shuffle, drag.

The old limp.

"Twenty-six." *It was Mum.*

"Yes, officer. Twenty-six." *It was Dad.*

Shuffle, drag.

"Thank you. Now, in the presence of Nurse Gail, and our orderly here Charlie, and I'm also recording this on my mobile device, I can declare that the face on the photograph you have provided, though dated three years ago, does show an approximation of David's face. Though, well, the damage caused by the explosion is not insignificant. But you have also positively identified a diamond of small moles on the right back of our patient, something I think only someone who intimately knew David would know."

"It's Ad. If you could take that tube out, you'd see an exact match with that photo." *It was Mum.*

"It's Adam, officer." *It was Dad.*

"Sorry. Adam. And you can address me as Detective Chief Inspector Pierce. Or DCI Pierce, if it's easier for you.

"Mr and Mrs Pound, please do not take this the wrong way, but we have had many crank calls, as well as some people actually in the room here with your son who have claimed to be in some kind of relationship with him. Can I ask you, perhaps, for one more form of identification? Any birthmarks? Or other scars?"

Silence.

"Geoff?" *It was Mum.*

"Okay, yes, he has scars on his feet. Idiot knocked over the kettle when he was little. Bare feet. Stupid boy, you know kids."

"I see."

"So, just take a look at his feet." *It was Dad.*

Silence.

"Sir. I'm afraid your son lost both of his lower legs in the explosion." *It was Nurse Gail.*

WHAT? I have no legs? Oh, Dillon, where are you? Why didn't you tell me? Get me away from these people. Get me away from you, Dillon. How can you care for someone so decrepit?

Sobbing.

"Oh Jesus, have mercy." *It was Mum.*

"Oh Adam, I can't believe it's you."

"Stop smothering him Valerie. Sit down, woman."

Sobbing.

Oh Mum. I'm sorry. So sorry you've found me. Forgive me, Mum.

"So, what do we have here then? Blooming police poking their noses in? What the hell they up to? Anyone can tell it's a jihadi attack."

Hateful Dad. You never change.

"Yes, Geoff."

"Adam, what were you even doing there? Piccadilly Circus, for goodness sake? You should have known. Why were you even up London? I thought you were at football. Even the train gets snarled up with those flags and whistles. The police prancing around with ribbons and shit. It's a disgrace. In my day, the police kept protests under control."

"I don't think he can hear you Geoff. That's what the doctor said."

"Jesus can hear, Valerie. Jesus can hear. Jesus knows why our boy got blown up by some jihadi. But I want to know why too. Adam, are you there at all?"

I'm here Dad. But I have nothing to say to you. I don't have to answer to you anymore.

"I hope you're praying in there, Adam. Praying for your sins, and for forgiveness in Jesus' name. We're praying aren't we, Valerie? For your recovery."

"Geoff, the doctor said..."

"And the doctors have not been touched by the hands of Christ, Valerie. We should take to our knees."

"Yes, Geoff."

"Join with us, Adam. Sweet Father, constantly help us to remember that You work in us according to Your good purpose. I know that You had a plan for Adam a long time ago, so everything in his life is happening for a reason. God, only You know that reason. Please help us to make it through this trying era in our life without questioning You. Help us to keep pushing through with strong faith and character. Keep our trust in You and don't let us become unmotivated. Make Adam and us fighters and give us the heart of a warrior. In Your name, I ask these things. Amen."

No Dad. Count me out. I have nothing to say to your God.

"Valerie?"

"Amen."

Dad, why would God do this to me? Why would He brutalise my body? Why would He take my legs? But you took my feet, didn't you Dad? The bomb blew them away, but you took them first. Washing them, you said.

Washing away my sins.

14

Knock.

Door.

"Hello, Mrs Pound. Mr Pound? David." *It was Dillon.*

Oh, thank God, it was Dillon.

"Doctor?"

"No, sorry. I'm not a doctor. My name is Dillon Kendrick. I'm from social services in Westminster. A volunteer actually."

"Social services. I've got nothing to say to social services. I want to talk to a doctor." *It was Dad.*

"No, sorry. Sorry to intrude. I've been allocated as David's responsible adult."

Caring voice, lovely man. Not like Dad. Not like Dad at all.

"Who's David? Responsible what?"

"Sorry, I'd hoped the doctor had explained."

"We haven't seen any doctors yet. Just nurses." *It was Dad.*

"When a person comes into hospital, and they're vulnerable, and can't be identified, the council allocates a responsible adult. Someone to look after David's interests, protect him if you like."

"Stop calling him David. His name is Adam."

"Protect him, from what?" *It was Mum.*

"Well, I guess to make sure no-one makes a decision about him or his needs, without proper consideration."

"Proper consideration? Look at him? What decisions need to be made about him. He needs medical help. Until he comes out of the coma."

"Sorry, Mr Pound. This must be quite a shock to you?"

"No, the only shocking thing is no-one called us earlier. We were away at a retreat. Only heard what happened when we got back. Adam wasn't home. Hadn't been for days. Next we know, he's here in a coma. After the Muslims blew him up. He was supposed to be at football."

"I'm so sorry, Mr Pound, Mrs Pound. It was a horrific day. You have my deepest..."

Such a lovely tone.

"Goodness knows what the police were doing even letting them march, in this climate."

"Climate, Sir?"

"Jihadis, son. They're looking out for crowds aren't they? Concerts. Trains. The gays should have stayed away. Setting themselves up as targets. Don't see why they can't keep themselves to themselves, anyway."

"Oh, so you didn't know about David. I'm sorry, it must have been a shock."

"David? Who's David?" *It was Mum.*

"Sorry, Adam."

"No, we were away, like I just said."

"Sorry, I mean, about him being at the Pride march."

"With the gays? Adam isn't gay. What are you talking about?"

I'm sorry Dillon. I'm not gay. I've tried to tell you. Sorry you had to hear it this way. I hope you're not disappointed.

"Oh, sorry, erm. I just assumed."

"Why on earth would you assume that? We're Christians, Mr Kendrick. Adam is a good Christian boy. He plays in the church band. Are you not a Christian, Mr Kendrick."

"Sir?"

"Geoff, leave it. It's not our business." *It was Mum.*

"No, hold on. You're his responsible adult. Or were. How do they allocate you people?"

"I'm very sorry, Mr Pound. I'm just a volunteer."

"Hold on. Oh, goodness, you're one of them aren't you? What you doing here, son? Getting your kicks from being around my boy."

"Sir, I can assure you I am a volunteer."

"Yeah, a volunteer on the recruit."

"Geoff."

"Let me make things clear to you, Mr Responsible Adult. You are no longer in charge of my son. He is not gay. I don't know how he ended up at Piccadilly Circus, but he definitely wasn't there to *celebrate*, if that's what you lot call it.

"And he got caught up in it when some jihadi blew up who knows how many innocent tourists and decent law abiding, God-fearing people. All I know is, it's time for you to leave. And keep your hands off my son."

I'm sorry Dillon. My dad is a shit. Please come back. Come back when he's not here.

Door.

You bastard. You bullying bastard.

"Ah, Mr and Mrs Pound, I'm glad you are here."

"Sorry, remind me who you are?" *It was Dad.*

"Dr Ann Atwan. I'm in charge of your son's care."

"Fine, I've seen you around. I thought you were a nurse. You've been looking after our boy?"

"Well, myself and my staff, yes."

"Your staff?"

"Yes, junior doctors. Nurses."

"I see."

Dad, you fucking racist. You misogynist.

Silence.

"So, Doctor, how's my son's recovery going? What are you doing to help bring him out of this coma?"

"Sorry, Doctor, my husband and I are just concerned. No pressure. We just feel..."

"That we're not being kept in the loop here, and we're his parents."

Dad the bully. Always the bully.

"Well, Mrs Pound, Mr Pound, I'm sorry you feel that way. If you'd like to take it up with my seniors..."

"No, no, carry on Doctor."

"Thank you, Mrs Pound. So, I wanted to fill you in on your son's condition."

"His recovery?" *It was mum.*

"May I take a seat? On Adam's bed, perhaps?"

I wish I could feel you sitting there Doctor. Your voice is so reassuring.

"This isn't very comfortable, but I wanted to talk to you both about your expectations about your son, and his recovery."

"We're Christians, Doctor. I suspect you are a religious woman yourself?"

"Sir, I wanted to manage those expectations for you a little. I've been with David, sorry, I've been with Adam since he first came into the hospital. I've monitored his condition the whole time."

Silence.

"Mrs Pound, Mr Pound, I'm afraid to say your son is very unlikely to recover from this state. The explosion not only caused the physical damage you have seen, his head, his face and torso, but he suffered what we regard as catastrophic head injuries."

"He's just sleeping."

Tears.

"I'm afraid not, Mrs Pound."

"It's just a coma, people recover from comas all the time." *It was Dad.*

"Mr Pound, I'm afraid you've been misinformed. Your son is in what we call a permanent vegetative state. He has no senses whatsoever, no feeling, no hearing, no sight, no taste. And we've carried out a number of tests. I'm sorry, your son is not even cognitive."

"Please, speak English Doctor."

"Sorry, I mean, your son is not even aware he is alive. And I'm afraid he's vulnerable to passing away at any time. He has already undergone three heart attacks - his brain is hardly in control of his organs. As his muscles continue to degenerate, that will become more and more likely. His lungs are likely to be affected too."

Sobbing.

"I'm sorry, would you both like a moment."

"Get it over with, Doctor Atan."

"It's Atwan. Sir, it is my opinion, and the hospital management's opinion, that we should allow David to pass away here in hospital, among the comfort of his family and the team who have treated him."

"How many times?"

"Sorry?"

"His name is Adam!"

"I am really very sorry."

Sobbing.

"See what you've done, Doctor? You've made my wife cry. Let me get this right? Plain English, if you even speak it? You want my son to die?"

"Sir, it's not what I want. It's my professional opinion."

"Awarded by whom? Because, last time I was at church, we listened to the Lord our God and what His plan was for His children. Or maybe that's not how it works wherever you go?"

"I am speaking as a doctor, Mr Pound. Mrs Pound. My clinical team and I have agreed, if your son does not recover in the next two months - which is very unlikely - then he should..."

"Be murdered? Listen, Doctor. My son has sins. We all have. And perhaps he is being punished right now, but we as Christians believe in forgiveness. We believe in repentance. God willing, there will be a miracle. Our son will come back to us, like Jesus Christ came back from the dead. Amen."

Sobbing.

"Valerie?"

"Amen."

"Mr Pound, I think you might like to take some time with your wife to discuss this further. My professional opinion is that your son will not recover. He will remain in this state, and this state will worsen. He could pass away at any time. We would spare him, and you, the suffering."

"Pah, professional opinion. You may look to medicine and all your mumbo jumbo, but I look directly to God and I have faith that He knows what is good for my son. He may pass away, he may recover. It is a sin for us, and for you Doctor, to assume superiority above our Father in heaven."

"Sir, that is your position and I respect that. I will go back to my managers, and report. It will be for them to decide where we go from here. I'm sorry we can't find common ground. Thank you for your time."

"Sure."

"Thank you Doctor."

"Thank you Mrs Pound."

"Oh Doctor." *It was Mum.*

"Yes, Mrs Pound."

"It's the tube. Isn't it hurting him? Does it go all the way down his throat?"

"I can assure you it's not hurting him."

"But my poor Adam. I want to see his face. And the sound, the gurgling. I can't stand it. He's my little boy."

Tears.

"Let me see what I can do, Mrs Pound. There are a number of ways we can feed him."

"Oh, thank you Doctor. I want to see him as he was. My beautiful boy."

"Of course."

Door.

Sobbing.

"Oh, Adam. My boy, Adam."

"Oh, do be quiet Valerie. I need to think."

15

"Well, good morning David." *It was Nurse Gail.*

"Let's get you sorted out, shall we? Mind if we pop the TV on?"

Gail. Nice voice. My guardian angel. Yes, I like listening to the TV.

Welcome back to the Sunshine Sofa, and we're lucky enough this morning to have our own political editor Natasha Harding in from the cold and enjoying a more leisurely time on our sofa with a cup of coffee. Good morning Natasha.

Good morning.

And with Natasha, we have Aaron Dixon, deputy editor at The Times.

Good morning.

So, Natasha it's all about the Piccadilly Bombing again, but we're starting to see that situation being rounded up?

Yes, Isha, take The Mercury's headline this morning: Saudi Satisfaction as Burka Bomb Probe Complete. It's looking like the government want this all to go away. And it looks like Foreign Secretary Dominic Hall has managed to placate the Saudis with the news that the Met has identified the suspect.

Dominic Hall has also declared that the initial findings from the Met were that it could have done better to pin down the perpetrator earlier.

Thanks Natasha. That'll please the Saudi Royals. Aaron Dixon from The Times?

Thank you, Isha. It's all very convenient, isn't it? But my sources tell me that the police are actually continuing to examine both the bombing, and their own investigation. My source is incredulous that the Minister has publicly reported the job is complete.

So not an end to the story?

I think this has a long way to run. We may well hear more from them in the next few days.

Thanks, Aaron. And now, things are also changing with regard to David, or is it now Adam, at St Michael's hospital. You'll remember, this is the sad case of a man who has been left in a vegetative state by the bomb? His parents have turned up, is that right Natasha?

That's right, Isha. The parents, Valerie and Geoff Pound have asked for their son to be called by his real name, Adam Pound.

They have asked for privacy. But at the same time, Geoff Pound has condemned both the police and the gay community for staging the Pride Festival at all. He says he blames the bombings on a combination of, and I quote, 'evils from across society'.

Aaron Dixon from The Times?

Well, I can only point to our own editorial this morning. 'David is being caught up in the grubbiest of battles, between politics, race, religion and dogma. It is time for this poor man to be given freedom to die in peace.'

Thank you, Aaron. And Natasha, that's another issue isn't it? David's right to die. It's one that hasn't really come to a head yet?

Well, yes, Isha. Taking a look at social media for a moment, a debate is beginning over whether Adam should be allowed to die in hospital. Some are defending doctors, who would allow the man to pass away, while others are supporting the Pound family, who are insisting - we understand - doctors keep him alive for the foreseeable future.

Aaron Dixon?

Ultimately, if it goes to court, it could be months or even years before a decision is made. There is precedence with Tony Bland, who you may remember was in a permanent vegetative state following the Hillsborough football stadium disaster in 1989. It took four years for the courts to decide the man should be allowed to die, and that was with the agreement of his parents. My paper will certainly be on the side of the doctors in this matter.

Well, thank you Natasha Harding. And Aaron Dixon from The Times, and now we're onto the weather...

"Oh, you poor, poor man."

It's okay, Nurse Gail. I don't mind. Let them score their points. There's nothing left for me.

"Must say, David, your dad seems a bit, well, strict. At least you've got some support out there? People standing up for their rights. For your rights, too David? I'd be out there too, if - well, I'd get into trouble wouldn't I? - in uniform and that.

"Hospital management wouldn't like it. But, I swear David, if it wasn't for my job, I'd be right there standing up for you too."

Door.

"David, it's Dillon."

Oh, I'm glad it's you.

"David, can I still call you David? I don't have much time. I wanted to pop in to see you, before I go."

Go where? I wanted to ask you something.

"I wanted to say goodbye. It's looking like your family are going to be making decisions about you now, so I've been released. They seem nice..."

You're sweet, Dillon. And a bad liar. They're not nice. You know it is not true.

"I'm sure they've got your best interests at heart. But I wanted to see you."

I think I'm gay, Dillon. I can finally say it. In this state, I can finally be free. You've helped me to realise he can't stop me.

"I guess I wanted to tell you that I wish you the best."

Dillon, be quiet. Don't go.

"I wanted to say good luck."

I'm gay, Dillon. It's such a release to say it. You could be my boyfriend.

"So, that's all really. I hope things go well for you."

Say you will?

"I know lots of people talk over you, but I want to tell you. Funny, I still don't know if you can hear me?"

I can. You're all I have.

"The doctors, they want you to pass away. They say there's nothing in there. And the kindest thing would be to let you die. And your folks? Well, you know your dad, I guess. They're disputing that. Your dad thinks there's going to be a miracle. That you'll come back to life.

"They have responsibility for you, but there's going to come a point when a judge has to decide. I'm afraid David - I hope you don't mind me still calling you David - it's going to be ugly. Protests. Appeals. And probably all played out in the media. It's not fair, you've been through so much. And the worst thing is..."

Are you crying, Dillon?

"The worst thing is. I can't do a thing. You can't do a thing about your own future. I don't know what you want. It was my responsibility, and I've failed you David. I'm not even supposed to say goodbye."

Don't go.

"The judges will have to decide, David. I hope they're fair. And they really do what's best for you. I have my own thoughts, but I can't burden you any further. I'd like to do more, but I have to do my job. It's been, well, something special."

Don't go. Please, I need you to tell them about Dad. Someone needs to tell the judge about Dad.

Did I just hear you kiss me?

"Take care, David."

Kiss me again. Please. On the lips. I want you to kiss me again. I want to kiss you back. Don't go, Dillon. Please, don't leave me alone.

Door.

"Hey, hey, that man!"

"Oh, God, what did those Mussies do to you?"

"They blew off your fucking legs man."

"Jesus."

"Guys, guys. Just chill. This is a hospital."

"Ad, can you hear us?"

"Quit messing."

"Can he hear us?"

I can hear you. I don't know who you are but I can hear you.

"Shit, we should have brought flowers or something. Hey, Ad, your dad said you were here. We had no idea. Thought you were off in Spain or something. Didn't turn up to footy."

"So sorry to hear it, man. You got caught up in that Parade. Fucking bad luck, man."

"Yeah."

"Anyway, your dad says you're on the mend."

"Don't look like it. The news said the doctors don't think..."

"Shut up Squirrel. He don't need to hear that. Look, he's breathing by himself. You in there, Ad? We're all rooting for you, mate. Down the Rose and Crown."

"Yeah, we got a banner up and everything."

"Mate, I swear, the moment you're back on your feet - well, you know - we'll wheel you down to the Rose, then go take in a game at Stamford Bridge."

"Hey, he'll get a special pass. Disabled or whatever."

"Yeah, we can all sit pitch side with you brother."

"Sweet as."

"Almost worth it, eh, Ad? Nah, only joking. Sorry about what happened to you mate. Hope you're not in pain, in there. Don't worry, mate, there will be consequences."

"Yeah, there's a few lads kicking off in the Muslim areas already. Hashtag Blue Team."

"Too right."

Blue Team? What the hell is Blue Team?

"Fuck man, can't believe they did that to him."

"See you, Ad. We'll be back, though."

"Yeah, with grapes or something next time."

"More like a tinny."

"Ha, ha, ha."

Door.

Silence.

Dillon? Dillon, are you there? Who were those people? So loud. Like the explosion. So very, very loud.

16

Silence

"Ah, Mr Pound, Mrs Pound, I'm glad you are here. You've not been answering my calls." *It was DCI Pierce.*

"We're staying at our son's bedside." *It was Mum.*

"Well, if you are able, I'd like to have a private conversation with you both."

"Private? There's nothing you can say to us that our Adam shouldn't hear." *It was Dad.*

"Really, Sir, I'd prefer to have a private room. Perhaps to record the conversation."

"Are we under arrest?"

"Certainly not, Sir."

"Then come out with it. What's the problem, Officer?"

"It's Inspector. I am Detective Chief Inspector Pierce, and this, again, is my colleague DI Ling. We'd like to ask you some questions about your son."

"I don't see why, Officer."

"I'm DCI Pierce."

"Okay, DCI Pierce."

"We're just trying to get some background. Are you happy to proceed?"

"And you're sure you wouldn't rather go to a private room." *It was DI Ling.*

"Our son can hear anything you have to ask us." *It was Mum. Voice much kinder.*

"Thank you, Mrs Pound. Can you tell us a little about your son?"

"He was a good boy. Church going, though we didn't insist he come on the retreats with us. I wish we had now, poor boy. Always got on well at school. Everyone liked him."

Liar, Dad. Liar. I was a weirdo.

"And he played in the church band. Keyboards. He was very good." *It was Mum.*

"We wanted him to work in the church somehow, but God had different plans for our Adam. He's not really settled. Worked in coffee shops, and garages. He likes his football though, doesn't he Valerie? He's been playing regularly. We're very proud."

Liar, Dad. You've never seen me play. Wouldn't let me play until I was a teenager.

"That's where he was on Saturday. That's where he was supposed to be. Must have got caught up somehow in London."

"We've been on a retreat. We've felt able to leave Adam alone more and more." *It was Mum.*

"Sorry, your son's age is?" *It was DI Ling.*

"Twenty-six."

"And you've not been comfortable leaving him alone, in your own home?"

"The world is a cruel place, Inspector. All young people are subject to temptations. The internet. Predators. So called influencers." *It was Dad.*

"Like my husband says, he didn't really settle."

"Okay, let's move on. Why would Adam have been in London Piccadilly on that Saturday." *It was DCI Pierce.*

Silence.

You know why, Dad.

"I have no idea. He should have been at football practice. That's where he goes every Saturday."

"Which is local?"

"Yes, local to us in Tooting Bec. But we were on retreat. We trusted him." *It was Dad.*

"You trusted your 26 year old son to go to football practice." *It was DCI Pierce.*

"He's been, well, wayward."

"Can you be more specific?"

"Not following the Christian way. Skipping church."

"Drinking." *It was Mum.*

"Valerie!"

"It's true, Geoff. Tell the officer."

"Okay, he's been going to pubs. Drinking alcohol. Coming home drunk."

"And driving?" *It was DI Ling.*

"Of course not. David can't drive."

"Abusing people? Getting into fights."

"No."

"Drugs?"

"Absolutely not."

"Public littering?" *It was DCI Pierce.*

"You are making fun of us." *It was Dad.*

"Sir, drinking too much is not a crime for a 26 year old man. Some would argue it would be a crime not to."

"Not in our family, Inspector. We follow Christ, and aim to be pure in His likeness."

"So, you were on retreat and trusting Adam to go to football, and not to go to the pub?" *It was DI Ling.*

"I suppose so." *It was Mum.*

"But it looks as if his will was not strong enough?" *It was Dad.*

Silence.

"Mr Pound, does Adam have many friends?"

"In the church, yes."

"Outside of church? Say, in the pub?"

"I wouldn't know. I don't want him seeing those friends if he did. Too much temptation."

"But we can assume if he did go to the pub. Or a pub. Or maybe even a pub at Piccadilly Circus, well, some friend - even a church one - might have come forward after the explosion, and said: I think I might know him?" *It was DCI Pierce.*

Silence.

"Sir?"

"Well, clearly you lot haven't done your job properly if it took a week for us to realise Adam had been hurt. And he's our son. Letting out little leaks, like you were. You should have been more upfront about him."

"Sir, we were protecting him by not revealing too much."

Silence.

"Just a few questions left, shall I continue?"

"Go ahead."

"Okay. Mr and Mrs Pound, do you think, or do you know, whether your son is gay, or bisexual, or otherwise interested in men? Is there any reason why he should have been at the Pride Festival?"

"No, absolutely not. My son is a child of Christ."

"Geoff, calm down." *It was Mum.*

"Honestly, Inspector, throwing around accusations."

"It was a question, Sir."

"My son Adam would want nothing to do with those queers, and their infections and their disgusting unnatural behaviour."

"Okay. Thank you. Sir, did he have a girlfriend? Perhaps someone he was seeing in Piccadilly Circus that weekend?"

"No, not that I know of. He does most of his socialising around the church."

"He had friends in the pub, but we're over that now." *It was Mum.*

"So, no reason you know, why he should have been at Piccadilly Circus on that Saturday?"

"Not that I know of, and not that I would have allowed. Certainly not on Pride day."

"I understand, Sir."

"Are we done?"

"DI Ling?"

"Yes, I think so."

"Can we be alone with our son now?" *It was Dad.*

"Yes, Sir. That's fine. Thanks for your time."

Door.

Silence.

Mum? Dad? Are you there?

"Geoff?"

"What?"

"Why didn't you tell them?"

"Tell them what, Valerie."

"About Adam."

"About Adam, what?"

"About his being..."

"Don't say it, Valerie. He is not..."

"He is Geoff."

"Be quiet, woman. He went through the programme, again and again."

"Geoff, our son is gay."

"Valerie, you will not speak that way. He has repented for his sins. Our son is not gay. He has been lifted from that sinful life."

Dad?

Silence.

"Well, it doesn't matter now, does it Valerie. The poor boy is as good as dead."

Silence.

Dad, you know it. My God, you know it. I am gay. I'm gay and you finally admit it. After all you've done to me. You stole my life. Leave me now.

Leave me alone with my misery. Let me die.

17

Door

"This way Minister." *It was DCI Pierce.*

"Aha."

"And may I properly introduce you to Mr Geoff Pound, and Mrs Valerie Pound. And their son, Adam. And this is Doctor Atwan, who has been lead consultant on Adam's case. And Nurse Gail O'Connor. This is Francis Gardiner, from the Home Office."

"Pleased to meet you all. I'm genuinely sorry for this situation. I bring the greatest sympathies from my government."

"We appreciate your visit, Minister." *It was Dad.*

"Yes, so sorry for the delay in meeting you. Quite sensitive matters, I hope you understand."

"Yes, Sir."

Sucking up Dad. Stiff upper lip. Fucking creep.

"So, I'm visiting today to officially express my government's sympathy to Adam, and to your family Mr and Mrs Pound. And that I hope the Metropolitan Police can draw a line under this case, so that you are able to grieve properly. I hope that's okay. Detective Chief Inspector, can you confirm?"

"Sir, our investigations are ongoing." *It was DCI Pierce.*

"But I'm sure you can confirm with the Pound family here, that your main suspect, what was her name, Noor Hisham, died in the bombing?"

"Yes, Sir."

"Then, can we not please consider the matter is closed?"

"We're still dotting the I's and crossing the T's, Sir."

"Yes, yes. We must trace the influences on the bomber, and I expect a public statement to that effect. But, Mrs Pound, Mr Pound, I can assure you that justice can be seen to have been done with the suicide of Noor Hisham herself. I don't believe we're looking for any other suspect of substance. I hope that gives you some comfort at least. DCI Pierce?"

"No other suspects at this time, Sir."

"Will there be an inquiry?" *It was Dad.*

"I'm sorry, Mr Pound?" *It was the minister.*

"Into why that Muslim was allowed close to the parade? Why the parade was allowed to happen at all? The failure of police?"

"I'm sure the Met will be examining its own actions on the day. Is that correct, DCI Pierce?"

"Sir, it will be up to my superiors, but I'm sure there will be an analysis of the events running up to and including the bombing, and police actions. That would be protocol."

"There you go, Mr Pound. The police will be looking into it. Thank you so much for your patience, and again, our greatest sympathy."

"But no public inquiry? Someone needs to apologise. Take responsibility for what happened to my son."

"Yes, Mr Pound, you are totally right. With your support, I can assure you we will look into it."

"Look into it?"

"Of course. I am Minister for the Home Office, and shall report to my committees. I'm sure one of my colleagues will be in touch."

"Thank you, Sir."

"No, thank you for meeting me. And really, may I express again our sympathies for you. And for all families caught up in the attack."

"He's not gay." *It was Dad.*

"I'm sorry, Mr Pound?"

"If you're going to make a statement, or whatever, to a committee, or the media. Adam, he isn't gay."

"Geoff." *It was Mum.*

"Mr Pound, my government would have no issue with your son's sexuality."

"He isn't gay."

Dad, you're a fake.

"Sir? I know this must be very difficult for you."

"He isn't gay."

"I understand, Sir. Of course. DCI Pierce, I hope that is noted? I will make sure I don't imply anything with any statements I make. As far as my government is concerned, there was a terrorist attack on London and all of its communities. As you know, a prominent member of the Saudi royal family was killed while shopping."

"Yes, shopping. That's what Adam was doing. He was shopping. We are a Christian family, Minister."

"I understand, Mr Pound. In the meantime, DCI Pierce, I'd like a private word about how we can start to round up this affair. I do need to make a statement to the Commons."

"Yes, Sir."

"Mr Pound, Mrs Pound. Adam. Thank you for your time, and my sympathies again. Would you like to accompany me out, DCI Pierce? Doctor Atwan, good to meet you. Nurse."

Good afternoon, and welcome to Express News, I'm Sophie Horgan.

The Home Office Minister Francis Gardiner has appeared in public for the first time with the parents of Adam Pound, the man who remains in a permanent vegetative state after the 21st June bombing at London's Piccadilly Circus.

Our political correspondent Natasha Harding reports.

Thank you, Sophie. I'm standing outside of St Michael's hospital, one of the biggest hospitals in the capital, and the destination for many of the casualties of that terrible bombing of the LGBTQ plus Pride Festival in June.

Adam Pound remains the only victim of that attack still in hospital. Eleven others were killed, and over 100 injured.

About half an hour ago, Home Secretary Francis Gardiner appeared on this lawn, with the parents of Adam Pound.

'I would like to express my deepest sympathy to the families and all the victims of the bombing. My thoughts are with Geoff and Valerie here, as uncertainty around their son's life remains.

'I am very glad the Metropolitan Police have brought this investigation to a close, as we can now allow all affected families to grieve.

'We stand together as Londoners to condemn any terrorist attack, or hate crime, on any members of our community. After this devastating bombing, I can reassure fellow citizens now that our government intends to crack down on social media companies, who have not done enough to stop extremist materials from being circulated. We will give the police more

resources to track down those who circulate such materials, and who attempt to take control of vulnerable young people.

'We're encouraging parents to keep a keener eye on what their children access online.'

Following the statement, Sophie, I questioned the minister about whether an independent inquiry into the bombing and its handling would take place.

'The police are carrying out their normal procedures, examining their response on the day. But this case is closed. I'm sure you'll see, as any upstanding British citizen can see, officers did their best on the day, and that the terrorist event could not have been predicted.'

Minister Gardiner said he would make a statement in the House of Commons tomorrow, but would not be recommending any new legislation. Back to the studio Sophie.

Thank you, that was our political editor Natasha Harding. In the studio now, we have Dean Joyce our special correspondent, who's been following the case closely. Dean, have we discovered anything new about the bomber?

Thank you, Sophie. As it is becoming clear, police suspect the bomber was Noor Hisham, a recent convert to Islam, who was also killed in the explosion. A statement from the Metropolitan Police said that Hisham was not previously known to them.

However there does seem to be a contradiction between what the police are saying about their investigations, compared with the Home Office as Natasha Harding just reported.

As far as we understand, the Metropolitan Police have not completed their investigation into the bombing.

Detective Chief Inspector Philippa Pierce, who is heading up the investigation, stated that she still welcomed any further footage, recordings or witness statements from the day...

18

It's night time. I'm used to the rhythm. The sounds of the hospital. Now a minimum.

I'm gay. It feels good to say that. Even though I can't feel anything.

Now it's all released. I can remember.

I feel, what is it? Unlocked.

Locked in, but unlocked.

Purgatory. Isn't that what you call it Dad? You wouldn't be pleased if I'd forgotten. I try to remember my lessons.

Purgatory.

The good, the sinless, those who mirror themselves after Jesus Christ. They go to heaven. And the sinful. The evil. Those unable to change their ways. The devil takes their souls to hell.

But those of us who try. Those of us who have the will to reject our sins. To ask for forgiveness. To atone for what we did wrong. We go to purgatory.

Renounce these feelings, and you may go to heaven. That's what you said, Dad. You have brought shame on our family, but you may yet be forgiven.

It was not enough. There were boys in my class I couldn't stop looking at.

Roger, the class show off. Watkins, the quiet boy with the artistic talent. Quick with a pencil, impressive with his modesty.

Lewis Harrison, a bulk of a boy already with a shadow of dark growing under a beautiful nose. He used a muscly arm to wipe the sweat away. Again and again, as he heaved his body this way and that on the rugby field.

Tight shorts, beautifully defined calf muscles. I'd sit with the rest of the class who were useless at sports. I'd watch him. Cross legged on the grass. My own school shorts more and more uncomfortable from the pressure rising up from below. But a pleasing feeling there, exactly where it rubbed.

I tried to look at the girls, but they were a different species. A world I didn't want to be part of. We passed each other in corridors, like cats pass each other in the street.

I'm not gay. I'm not gay.

That's what I had to repeat. In the programme. Day after day after day.

I'm not gay. I'm not gay. As if repeating the words took away the desire.

Repent!

A big word. Dad, you said it all the time. Repent for your sins. Repent for your feelings. Repent for cursing. Repent for our shame. Repent for not repenting. Repent for existing.

Repent for being gay. Repent for getting a hard-on while watching Lewis Harrison run with the ball, and dive towards the try line, his taut thighs rubbing against the grass, forcing his shorts up and into the tight balls of each of his ass cheeks.

Repent! Repent for homo-sex-ual acts.

Repent? I hadn't done anything. God I wanted to. Whatever homo-sex-ual acts were. Dad, I didn't know. There was no-one to do them with, anyway.

Lewis, and Roger, and Watkins, but only in my mind. Under the covers into the night, where I held myself, unsure of why or what to do with it.

In a sense, Dad, you were responsible for that. Even the thought of homosexual acts. You gave what I was feeling a name. And an end goal.

Homosexual acts.

I'm not gay.

I wasn't, Dad. Not until you put me on the programme. Me and three others from the church. A pastor, travelled from up north. We went to a house in the country.

Pastor Priest. We laughed at the name. Me, and Mark Derrin and Unan Megawaty.

None of us were gay, Dad. Pastor Priest made us say it.

Me: I'm not gay.

Mark: I'm not gay.

Unan: I'm not gay.

We read passages from the Bible. Leviticus 2:3, Acts: 12:34.

We asked God for forgiveness. We promised to repent for our sins, Dad. Though none of us had done any sinning. None of us had done any homo-sex-ual acts.

I'm not gay. I'm not gay. We were forced to say it when we wore that crown of thorns.

I'm not gay. I'm not gay. When we were forced to carry that cross around the forest.

I'm not gay.

And then, in the night, when me and Mark Derrin and Unan Megawaty were bunked together, in the dusty room of that country house, all sweaty with the day's heat, and scary with spider webs, we comforted each other. Said kind words. Invited each other into our beds. Told ourselves we would get through this. Together. May the Lord be with us.

And then we'd take care of each other's desires. Explore every inch of each other's bodies. Just as we'd explored our own.

We were not gay.

We told ourselves that as we prayed with Pastor Priest. We were not gay, we told each other, as the pastor forced us to cane each other. We were not gay, we declared to Jesus and to God, as we walked laps of the forest, naked, nettles bringing our souls and our soles into punishing blisters.

We were not gay. But in the night, we did homosexual acts.

And I can say, now Dad. Now that I am free of you. I'm glad. I'm glad I got to discover my body and Mark Derrin's body and Unan Megawaty's body.

The punishments were worth it, because when I'd learned what a joy homosexual acts could be, what a flutter to my heart they could bring, I could go out and do them for real.

In beds. In the woods. In the top floors of dingy nightclubs. In my bedroom at your house, Dad. Like any normal horny teenager.

And once, only once, there in that church cupboard where they keep the extra chairs for Easter and Christmas. Next to where the band plays. Oh, yes. Sinful sex at church. And you wouldn't believe who with. Oh, you wouldn't believe it.

But Jesus knows. Isn't that what you would say, Dad? The Lord God our Father knows. Our sinful acts. Our sinful thoughts. Well, if I am in purgatory, I don't see that faithful friend from church around these parts.

I don't see a thing. Ha, ha, ha.

So really, Dad. I have you to thank for that, don't I. This purgatory, if that's what you call it? This darkness. This loneliness.

My son isn't gay! What a lie, Dad. It was thanks to you I gave in to the temptation. I learned the joy of giving in to the pleasure of homo-sex-ual acts.

It's called sex, Dad.

Sex.

Gay sex. And do you know what? There's not one thing a gay couple can do that a straight couple can't. Ever thought about that, Dad? Not one thing.

Whatever you've tried to do to me, however you tried to punish me, now I am free from you. Lying here with no legs, and a face scarred with glass and fire, I can finally say it: I am gay.

And there's nothing you can do about it.

The Foreign Secretary Dominic Hall is expected to make a statement to the House of Commons this afternoon, about his recent visit to Riyadh, where he offered personal sympathy to the Saudi royal family. Our political correspondent Natasha Harding reports.

Thank you, Sophie. Mr Hall is due to make a statement to the House around three this afternoon. Indications are that he will state that relationships with Saudi Arabia are good, and that the UK government looks forward to long and continued relationships with the state.

Remember, a member of the royal family, Prince Yusuf Al-Ghamdi, was killed in the June attack.

It is expected that the minister will state that the Saudis have been assured the Metropolitan Police have concluded their investigations.

Throughout this affair, the Foreign Secretary has sought to play down reports of tensions between the British government and Saudi Arabia, over the London Piccadilly Bombings.

Business leaders had warned damage to British-Saudi relationships might hurt contracts for aerospace...

Click.

Silence.

"Oh, dear. Poor David." *It was Doctor Atwan.*

"Doctor?" *It was Nurse Gail.*

"Sorry Nurse. It all gets a bit much."

"No, go ahead, I know what you mean."

"It's been two weeks since the bombing, and only now a hint of sympathy from the government for David? Now he's out there, with the family, the Met, having his picture taken with our hospital logo."

"Are you okay, Doctor?"

"You were on shift that day, Gail. You saw the carnage. People bleeding in the corridors. We ran out of beds. Turned ambulances away. I didn't sleep for two days. The police crawling all over my patients."

"I remember."

"It gets to you. The lack of appreciation. When you're, well when you're an Arabic woman. They've really no idea how hard it was to get to where I am. In Saudi, I'd have to have worked twice as hard."

"Do you mind if I ask where you *are* from?"

"Yemen, Nurse. So, you'll understand why I'm not exactly keen on the Saudis. But the British government are worse. They pretend to care, but bend over backwards for the Saudi royals. David here, he's just small fry compared to a big arms deal."

"He's called Adam, Doctor."

"Yes, but we know him as David. Don't we?"

19

Door.

Loud voices.

"What's this about, officer, I really am very busy."

"Thank you for seeing me, Doctor, it's most urgent." *It was DCI Pierce.*

"Come in, Gail."

"Are we okay, to talk in here?"

"Yes, Detective Chief Inspector."

"Where's that Kendrick, volunteer representative or whatever?"

"He's been stood down. The parents have come back, so he has no jurisdiction."

"I see."

"So, what's this all about, Inspector?"

"Well, we wanted to warn you. There's about to be a shit storm, and I wanted to let you know, and I guess the family too. And maybe we should have some kind of media strategy." *It was DI Ling.*

"What's happened?"

What's happened? Where's Dillon?

"It's Noor Hisham."

"The bomber?"

"Yes, only *not* the bomber."

"What? But you said."

"No, we didn't say. We quite specifically didn't say. The Minister said it. We suspected it, but everything else was leaked. We continued the investigations. And now we have conclusive proof that Charlotte Brookes, aka Noor Hisham, couldn't have done it. She definitely died in the blast. But she didn't cause the bomb."

"And what has this got to do with us at the hospital, Detective?"

"Only that every Tom, Dick and Harry reporter is going to be knocking at that door, followed by a very angry Geoff Pound and an even angrier Home and Foreign Office, as soon as we drop this news."

"Shit."

"The bomber might still be out there. Expect more people trying to get news on Adam, even trying to get new photos. You'll have a press pack at the door again. If you'd hoped this was going to go away, and you'd be back to normal business, you're mistaken. There are likely to be more protests, and an even bigger vigil.

"All eyes are going to be on Adam again as the only surviving victim, and there will be renewed calls for the Met to do a better job for his family. Plus more pressure from the Saudis about the death of their prince not being solved. They'll be furious, and the government will be desperate to appease them - very desperate.

"Any hopes of allowing Adam to quietly pass into the night are a long way off, Doctor Atwan. You better prepare yourself and your staff for a much longer ride."

Door.

"Hello Adam, just in to change your sheets. Come on Marj."

"He looks sad today."

"He looks sad everyday."

"Okay, Adam, and we lift. That's good."

"Did you hear? About the bombing, Marj?"

"What bombing?"

"What bombing? The one that injured poor David here."

"Adam."

"Yeah, Adam. I heard about it on the radio on the way in this morning. The police chief was on, that Pierce woman. Turns out the bomber wasn't that Muslim woman after all."

"My goodness, Sheila. Poor girl. Poor David."

"Yeah, okay, nice and slow, down, down, down. Do you want to do the toilet, and I'll wipe down the surfaces."

"So."

"Go on, Sheila."

"The police chief said they'd done more investigations into the white Muslim's background. You know she was converted over the internet? Well, turns out - at least this is what I got from it - she was converted into, well, good Muslims not bad Muslims. I guess that's right."

"I'm saying nothing."

"Well, turns out she did lots of community work and things. And she was, well, part of like a modern Muslim clan or something. They called it progressive, whatever that means. Friendly to women. Gays and the like. Stands up against the fierce ones, Marj."

"Fierce gays?"

"No, fierce Muslims."

“Got any gloves.”

“Here you are. So, she was at the gay pride festival, or whatever, supporting the gay Muslims and the gay black people. She was giving out leaflets and that.”

“What did the police say?”

“That chief of police said new footage had come in showing her dancing, and messing about, and even leading the chants under that BLM banner.”

“BLM?”

“Black Lives Matter, you should know that Marjorie.”

“Oh, yeah. So she was supporting them?”

“Police say she was well known to the BLM people. And when the bomb went off, she was with them.”

“Not a suicide bomb, then?”

“No, Marj, because, you see, she’s not carrying anything. That’s what the police say. She’s got this placard in her hands. She didn’t have a bag or a rucksack or anything.”

“She could have had something under her gown or whatever.”

“The police said not. Dunno how they know that, maybe something to do with the autopsy.”

“Grim.”

“Pass me that cloth. So, anyway, I hear the police chief on the radio, she says that this Noor Hisham, she picked up a bag.”

“Oh, the bomb. So she did do it.”

“No, listen, she saw a bag on the floor. That’s what the footage shows, this police woman says. She saw it, dropped the placard, then went to pick it up - maybe it was lost or whatever - and the moment she touched it.”

“Oh, horrible.”

“Horrific, Marj.”

"Poor woman. Worst of luck, not only to be blown apart..."

"Marjorie, not appropriate."

"Sorry, not only to have suffered, but also, well to be blamed for it. The whole bombing."

"I know, such a shame."

"She was doing a good thing. Trying to find someone who'd lost their bag. Exactly the opposite of what they said about her. No justice. I reckon her dad must be really fuming."

"You know who should be cross?"

"Who Sheila."

"Our David here."

"Adam."

"Yeah. Poor man. Doctors and police had it all sewn up. Justice, you know? And now where for him?"

Flushing sound.

"Are we all done, Sheila?"

"Just perk up these flowers. That's nice."

"Beautiful."

"Okay, Adam, see you tomorrow."

And you join us now as Home Office Minister Francis Gardiner is about to make a public statement on the 21st June explosion at the London Pride Festival.

Our political editor Natasha Harding is at the Home Office awaiting the press conference. Natasha, what can we expect just now?

Thank you Sophie. Well, what we are about to hear, I think, will be of no surprise to those who've seen the headlines from much of this morning's press.

Word around Westminster is that Francis Gardiner will backtrack on what was once government certainty that 15 year old Noor Hisham was the bomber at the parade during the summer.

And that will be quite a climb down from the government's previous position, Natasha?

Yes, Sophie. Downing Street will want to stay as far away from this as possible, which is why I think we're hearing from the Home Office today. The Metropolitan Police fall directly under the auspices of the Home Office, though it is clear that relations have not been good in recent months.

It now seems certain that Noor Hisham, a 15 year old schoolgirl recently converted to Islam, did not carry out the bombing. My understanding was that the Metropolitan Police had been keeping an open mind on the issue, and was still investigating. The Home Office, perhaps, was not so patient.

Oh, Mr Gardiner is about to take the podium. We can now go live to the statement from the Home Office to hear a statement from Dominic Hall.

'... of the press, ladies and gentlemen, thank you for joining us today. I'd like to start, once again, by expressing my and my government's deepest sympathy for the victims of the awful events of 21st June in London. Our hearts go out to the families affected.'

Click. Click. Click.

'Thank you. Thank you. Our government is committed to fairness and equality in this country, and I can reassure all that intolerance of any kind will not be, er, tolerated.'

Click. Click.

'So, ahem, please bear with me.'

Click. Click.

'I'm here this afternoon to reassure the public that through close working with the Metropolitan Police, that we will further

be pursuing the perpetrator or perpetrators of this heinous crime. More evidence has come to light, and we've allocated more resources to the investigations into the events of 21st June.

'I have personally pledged whatever resources are needed for Detective Chief Inspector Pierce at the Metropolitan Police to finally get to the bottom of this matter.

'At the same time, I can announce that we have asked the Metropolitan Police to launch an internal investigation into the mistakes that were made in their investigations of the bombing so far, including the delay in bringing the correct perpetrator to justice. The inquiry will be reporting directly to me, according to a deadline I have set.

'We deeply regret any further grief these delays have created. I have met personally with the families of some of the victims and others deeply affected by the events, and once again express my own and the government's deepest sympathies.'

Click. Click.

'I am afraid that these ongoing investigations are classified, and I cannot fairly speak of them any further, in order not to prejudice any investigation or findings to follow. I hope members of the press will understand, and you will all be provided with a copy of this speech, as well as some background inform...'

Minister, Minister...

'I'm sorry, I will not be taking questions.'

Sir, are you under pressure from the Foreign Office?

'Thank you. Thank you for coming.'

Minister, do you have anything to say to the family of Noor Hisham...

Sir, will you apologise to the Muslim community?

Click. Click.

'Thank you, that is all I have time for this afternoon.'

Silence.

Okay, we're back again at Express News. I'm Sophie Horgan. We have just returned from a short, live statement from Home Office minister Francis Gardiner regarding the bombing of the LGBTQ plus pride festival on 21st June.

We didn't quite expect that to go so quickly, but I think, yes, I think we go back to our political editor Natasha Harding, who is at the Home Office right now. Natasha, what's your analysis?

Well, Sophie, quite a revelation this afternoon in what was not said by the Home Office minister just now.

There was no mention of Noor Hisham, and no clarity about what any further investigation will be concentrating on. I think we did learn that the Metropolitan Police have been asked to investigate - was it - investigate themselves? Though the minister wasn't very clear about what that investigation was supposed to be looking into.

The minister also announced that he would be providing 'whatever resources are needed' to the Metropolitan Police to, as he put it, 'finally get the job done'. Some tension, there, I'm detecting between the Home Office and the Police.

Thank you, Natasha. And if you've just joined us, we've just heard from the Home Office minister...

Click.

"That just makes me crazy, Gail."

Doctor Atwan. I was asleep. Is that you Nurse?

"Doctor?"

"The Minister. Gardiner, he's as swervie as they come. Won't apologise for getting it wrong about Noor Hisham. The Saudis will be hopping mad, but I knew something didn't add up. That poor girl."

"How do you mean?"

What's going on Doctor?

"Well, I knew she wasn't the one. Her dad was so sincere.

No way, I thought. I mean, it would have been a pretty awesome feat for a 15 year old girl. She didn't just walk into a hardware store and ask for a sack of assorted nails and a litre of acetone peroxide."

"She'd have needed a lot of hate." *It was Nurse Gail.*

"Yeah, that too. And from such a stable family? Her family was a safety net for her. Gave her the space to be herself. I couldn't do that with my daughter. And my dad didn't let me."

Dads can be animals, Doctor Atwan. They say they do it to protect us, don't they?

"Didn't the police have good evidence?"

"They had motive to pin it on Noor Hisham. Or at least the Home Office did. The Saudis baying for blood. The government blames it on a Muslim, only not a *real* Muslim. Very useful, that. Keeps in with that community. And she died in the blast. All done and dusted. Very convenient."

"That's very cynical, Doctor."

"And the media did their duty didn't they? Pinned that girl to the wall. Camped outside her poor parents' house. Didn't give them a chance to grieve."

"So, does that mean the police and media will be back here?"

"I don't know. The government will be under severe pressure, that's for sure. It'll be gorgeous."

"Doctor?"

"Watching them squirm, Gail. Watching them squirm."

"Poor David. He didn't deserve any of this. It's hard not to have a soft spot for him. His folks are so awful." *It was Nurse Gail.*

"Nurse, that's enough. For both of us, I think. Good job that Mr Kendrick isn't here. He'd have us up in front of social services for talking that way."

Laughing.

Ha, Doctor Atwan. I never knew you had a sense of humour.

Silence.

"Thanks, Gail. It's good to lighten the load a little."

"Yeah, thanks Doctor. It's been pretty rough."

"I'll see you out."

20

"Are you awake, my darling?"

"Leave him be, Valerie."

"He is awake. I can feel it."

"Nonsense, don't fuss."

I must have been asleep. Is Dillon here?

"The pastor sends his regards." *It was Mum.*

"So, guess you've heard lad. Police reckon that Muslim girl didn't do it. Good Christian girl, turned bad by the internet. Who knows why she was down there on the protest."

"It was a march, Geoff."

"March, protest, same thing. Don't know what the gays were marching for. government already gave them everything they want: same sex marriage, for goodness' sake. Right to have kids. Adopt, even, Valerie."

"Anyway, I think we should focus on Adam."

Thanks Mum.

"Yeah, like why was Adam down there with the gays when he was supposed to be at football?"

"Geoff, can't you let it go?"

"He's lied before, Valerie. You've been too easy on him.

But God knows every sin."

"We should have been there for him more, Geoff."

"We were there. Taking him to church, putting family first, those who pray together, stay together."

No, Dad. It was too much. All I wanted was to be left alone. We could have agreed to disagree. I could have gone about my life, and you gone about yours. Turn the other cheek, Dad?

"It wasn't enough, Geoff."

I don't like being gay, Dad. All that flaunting about. The glitter. The limp wrists. It makes me sick. But I understand now. Not all gays are like that. And Dad, now they've been hurt? Maybe I'm ready to turn the other cheek. Live and let live. Why can't you do the same?

"Well, guess they'll have to find the other Muslims who did it. Because I want justice for my boy. So we can bring him home with pride."

"No one is saying it was a Muslim, anymore."

"Get real, Valerie. They hate us. They hate everything we stand for. I don't know why they're here, if all they want to do is destroy. I've no problem with them, but they can do their horrible little deeds in their horrible, dusty, God-forsaken places, as far away from us as possible."

Dad, get out. I don't want to hear you. I'm tired of you. You're horrible. I am no longer under your control. Go. Please. Just. Go.

"Geoff, calm down."

"Well, Valerie what am I supposed to think? My poor boy here on the bed. Not talking. Hurting.

"Because I'm hurting, Valerie. We've put so much into this boy. I love him. Where is he, Valerie. Where's my boy?"

"He's here, and by the grace of God, he'll stay with us." *It was Mum.*

"No, Valerie. He's gone. I lost him. I drove him away. Into the hands of..."

"No, don't say it."

"Into the hands of them. I made him gay, Valerie. I pushed him too hard. He rebelled and chose to be gay, just to resist me. Just to prove something. But I did it."

"It's okay Geoff, no need to cry."

Dad?

"I'm NOT crying, Valerie. I'm just, well, I'm just sad. It could have been different."

"It's okay, come here, husband."

"No, Valerie. It is time to pray."

"Can't we just have a moment together? Us three?"

"Us three and Jesus, Valerie. We should kneel."

"Do we have to?"

"Valerie!"

"Yes, Geoff."

"You lead, Valerie."

"I don't know what to say."

"Don't make me tell you again."

"Okay, sorry."

I shall never pray with you. You are one messed up man. I wish you would just leave.

"Our Father..." *It was Mum. Poor Mum.*

Knock.

Door.

"Get out." *It was Dad.*

"I'm sorry, do you have a moment." *It was Doctor Atwan.*

"We're praying. Join us, or go."

"Well, I'm not, you know."

"Then go. Five minutes, that's all I ask for. With my own son and wife."

"Yes, yes of course. Sorry."

Door.

"Continue, Valerie. Our Father..."

"Mr Pound, it's about Noor Hisham." *It was the doctor.*

"That Muslim woman? Charlotte, that was her Christian name, wasn't it?"

"I guess it was her birth name."

"Then we should call her Charlotte, her baptised name. They are a Christian family, as I understand it."

"Anyway. Her father, Peter Brookes, he's asked for a message to get through to you. He'd like to meet."

"What on earth for? I have nothing to say to him."

"The man is suffering, Mr Pound. Not only has he lost a child - just like you - but his daughter has been in the spotlight for a month as the bomber. I imagine this man just wants to, I don't know. Touch base. Clear the air."

"I have nothing to say to him. What kind of a father lets their child go to a gay pride protest? What kind of a father allows their child to be influenced by extremists. We have nothing in common with that man."

"Mr Pound, you may find it helps with the grief?"

"Grief? I have no grief. I have a very sick son, who is going to get better, if only you would do your job. You want him to die here. I know he will live. So, instead of trying to be little miss make-up-never-break-up, get on with being a doctor."

"Geoff?"

"No Valerie, I want to see justice, not hugs and kisses. What are the police doing to track down the Muslims who did this to my son? If it wasn't this man's daughter, then who was it? I reckon he knows more than he's letting on. You can tell that to him. Come clean. And tell it to the police, too."

Oh, please, allow me to escape from this cruel man. Please, let me die. And let Dad rot in hell, for the rest of eternity.

21

Door.

"Please come in gentlemen, please come in." *It was Dad.*

"Oh Lord God have mercy, is that really Adam?"

I know that voice.

"Yes, Pastor. My son, Adam."

"God bless you child, in the name of the Father."

"Amen."

"Amen."

"Amen."

"Amen."

No, it can't be. Please, say it's not.

"Well, well, let's have a closer look at you. Oh, brother Geoff, you have the blessings of the church and our deepest sympathy."

"Please, Pastor Priest, will you take his hand?"

No, please tell me no.

"Of course, Brother Geoff. Can he hear me?"

Get away from me.

"We'd like to think so, we're not sure. The doctors say

not, but I believe Jesus Christ will find a way through to him."

"I believe that too, my son."

"Amen."

"Amen."

"Amen."

"Amen."

Take your amens away from me.

"Pastor, I am told that my son will remain in this wretched state, and may pass away at any time. But I believe, with the Lord Jesus' mercy, he may be forgiven his sins and be allowed to repent."

"It is for the Lord to decide, Brother Geoff, whether your son will recover from this state."

"Pastor, I hope that we will be able to pray for him, to appeal upon Highest for this man to be given a second chance."

"Another chance, Brother Geoff? I think we have petitioned our Lord many times on behalf of your son. Our God is faithful and patient, but our lives go by His grace not our whims."

"Amen."

"I understand, of course. But, we can still pray for him. In sympathy. With our hearts open. My son, Pastor, he is still my son. My wife and I love him. He has done wrong, but what parent can reject a child?"

Dad, what is this? Is this really you?

Silence.

"We shall pray for his soul, Brother Geoff. But his fate will be decided by Lord God alone. We will not petition for mercy, as we have before."

"Please, Pastor Priest, if I may? We have lived our lives for the church. We brought our son, Adam, into the church for christening. He attended church nursery school, he was baptised by the very holy water you blessed. My son played in the church band. He was not a bad child."

Dad, are you begging? Are you begging for me?

"And when he became wayward, did he not come willingly to your programme for correction? Time and again. He never refused. He wanted to be cured of his illness. He wanted to learn the error of his ways."

"This is true." *It was the pastor.*

"He tried Pastor. He is a faithful man. He was in church on the day we last saw him. He has not missed a Sunday, nor a band practice, since... well, since his stay in the recovery centre. Does this not show his determination to be a better man? A Christian man?"

I did try, Dad. You're right. In the name of the Lord I tried. I did everything I could. And more than you can ever know. But please, don't beg for me. I don't deserve that. I can see your pain now.

"Enough, Brother Geoff. Let us kneel, gentlemen. Let us kneel in silence, pray, and be patient on God's will."

Shuffling.

Oh, my God. Are you all surrounding me? Like before? With the other boys.

"Lord, we ask for direction in this most difficult of challenges. We know you are an all merciful God, but the Bible directs us to Your will. We ask for lightness in the darkness. Clarity in the gloom. We are forever in Your faithful service. Amen."

"Amen."

"Amen."

"Amen."

"Amen."

Dad, you can stop this. I don't need it. It's okay to be gay. I know that now. I know you can never accept it, but you can move on without me. Please, don't shame yourself in front of these men.

Silence.

Silence.

Shuffling.

"I am prompted to turn to the Holy Bible. Please turn your pages to John, chapter three."

Shuffling.

"Brother Stephen. Please read from verse four."

Oh, I know that chapter. I know it too well.

"Everyone who makes a practice of sinning also practices lawlessness; sin is lawlessness. You know that He appeared in order to take away sins, and in Him there is no sin. No one who abides in Him keeps on sinning; no one who keeps on sinning has either seen Him or known Him."

"Brother Elvin."

"Little children, let no one deceive you. Whoever practices righteousness is righteous, as He is righteous. Whoever makes a practice of sinning is of the devil, for the devil has been sinning from the beginning. The reason the Son of God appeared was to destroy the works of the devil.

"Brother Christopher."

"No one born of God makes a practice of sinning, for God's seed abides in Him; and he cannot keep on sinning, because he has been born of God."

"And Brother Geoff."

Silence. Sobbing.

"Brother Geoff."

"I can't. Please have mercy on his soul."

Dad, are you crying?

"Very well, I shall finish it myself." *It was the pastor.*

Shouting.

"By this it is evident who are the children of God, and

who are the children of the devil: whoever does not practice righteousness is not of God, Amen."

"Amen."

"Amen."

"Amen."

Sobbing.

"Lord thank You for Your direction, and Your ever merciful release of our burden. This man is still full of sin. The Lord our God may yet cast a graceful miracle over his soul. But without repentance, he is destined for the eternal fires of hades. Now, together, the Lord's prayer. Our Father…"

"Wait."

Sobbing.

"Wait? This is most unusual, Brother Geoff."

"Please, the Bible. The Word of God. Romans chapter fifteen, verse one."

No Dad, don't do that. Have courage. Like I now have courage.

"Go ahead, Brother Geoff."

"Romans chapter fifteen, verse one. 'We who are strong have an obligation to bear the weaknesses of those without strength, and not to please ourselves.'"

Dad, I am not your fault. You're not to blame.

"'Whoever spares the rod hates his son, but he who loves him is diligent to discipline him.' Proverbs twenty, verse thirty-four."

"I failed my son, Pastor. I deserve punishment, not him."

Dad, you don't have to do this.

"Enough, Brother Geoff. You are saying you wish to take on the sins of your son?"

"I do, Pastor. You know the lessons I went through. I am grateful, but I have not succeeded in rescuing my son.

Matthew, eighteen, verse six. Jesus said 'whoever causes the downfall of one of these little ones who believe in Me - it would be better for him if a heavy millstone were hung around his neck and he were drowned in the depths of the sea.'"

"You understand what you are asking for?"

"Yes, to take the punishment due to my son, in order to receive the mercy of God for him."

Dad, don't do this. You don't need to. Walk away. Can't you see how warped all of this is? I'm not going to recover. You've been through what I have. You too were wayward. Drugs, Dad. Alcohol. I know all about it. Mum told me, don't you understand?

"Mmm, this is unusual."

I know about your leg injury Dad. I know what Pastor Priest did to you. He and your own father. You were just a teenager. Like with me, it made no difference.

"In the name of Jesus Christ, I offer myself at the complete mercy of God. I have money Pastor. Money for the church."

Dad, no. Stop this.

"Very well, this needs to be discussed with church elders. But I feel we may be able to find a way through."

"Praise be."

"Amen."

Sleep.

Click, whirr.

Click, whirr.

No, not the pictures. Not the pictures again. Please.

Look up, boys. Look. That's right.

No, please.

I said look up!

Kkkccc.

Aww. Aww. No, please.

Kkkccc.

Aww. Aww.

Look again. Look again at the pictures. Do you like them?

No, please. No more.

Kkkccc.

Aww. Aww. No, more.

Lord have forgiveness on their souls.

Now, look again.

No, please.

Look again!

Kkkccc.

Aww. Aww. Please.

Lord ...

Lord have forgiveness on our souls.

Again.

Lord have forgiveness on our souls.

Crying.

It's for your own good, boys. Look again.

No more. No more.

Kkkccc.

Awake.

What's happening? Is anyone there?

Nurse?

Dillon?

A dream. It was just a dream.

Sleep.

Door.

Shuffle, drag. Shuffle, drag.

"Well, a right bother we've got ourselves into here, son, haven't we?"

Is that you Dad?

"Your mum's taken a break. Can't deal with everything. But don't worry, Adam, we've got you back now."

No, Dad. I'm not yours.

"The doctors want to take you away from us Adam. Our son, our lovely son Adam. Can you believe that? Lord God created you, and they think they have the right. Oh, my boy, my boy."

Dad?

"I don't understand this, Adam. We have been faithful to God, all of us. We've prayed every day. Atoned for our sins. Is there something we've missed, Adam? We tried, didn't we? We tried so hard? And for it all to end up like this? Jesus suffered for our sins, and I'm trying..."

Dad, you are crying.

"I'm trying to understand, how could this have happen to us? God forgive us all, but God forgive me for failing Him. For failing you."

Dad?

"Listen, I know you can hear me. God knows you need to hear what I say. You are suffering, I am suffering too. We are paying our dues. But I want to say to you, Adam, I have to say it, here, alone, but under the watchful eye of Jesus Christ. I believe you did everything you could. To stop... to stop being gay."

What?

"I know you were not just passing that parade. I know you were there because it is something that is inside you. I cannot be proud of you, but I think I can understand. You could not do what Jesus asked of you. We worked hard, but the devil was strong.

"I just can't stand to lose you, my son."

Dad? I don't understand. Dad, don't cry. It's not your fault. You were brought up this way, too. You learned to be hard on me. On Mum. On yourself?

"I failed. Failed to rescue you from temptation. It's not your fault, Adam. I should be punished, and I will wait to discover what our Lord has planned. But you, my boy. My lovely boy. I need to ask for your forgiveness. God will not punish you. Like Jacob, let me take any punishment due to you, be bestowed upon my shoulders instead."

Dad, I did everything you asked of me. I tried so hard. At the programme. I tried so hard to obey your wishes. I was at the parade. I am so sorry. I am sinful.

Tears.

"Our Father in heaven, hallowed be Thy name. Thy Kingdom come, Thy will be done, on earth as in..."

Knock.

Door

"Oh, sorry." *It was Doctor Atwan.*

"Hi." *It was Nurse Gail.*

"We can come back."

"No, just taking a little quiet time with Adam. Please, help me up. Thank you."

"Sore legs, Mr Pound?"

"Just the one, an old rugby injury to the knee. Gives me that limp."

"Oh, I hadn't noticed."

How could you miss it, Doctor?

"So, what's the news Doctor?" *It was Dad.*

Gentle voice this time.

"Sorry, Mr Pound, I'm the nurse. This is the doctor. Doctor Atwan." *It was Nurse Gail.*

"Oh, yes, well, sorry."

Wow, Dad.

"Well, as stated, we regard your son as being in a vegetative state, but as far as the law allows, he is under your ward for the time being."

"And so he should be. He's my son."

"Sir, I'd like to step out of that debate. It will be for the hospital managers to decide the direction of that. For the time being, we'll keep your son in hospital and give him the treatment he needs."

"Well, as long as you consult me first."

"Indeed, Mr Pound. Now, I would like to begin some kind of occupational therapy for Adam. What that means is, a physiotherapist will come and lift his arms up and down, move his head around, twist his back and shoulders, stretch his neck. Otherwise, his bones will fuse and his muscles will wither. Your wife expressed concern about his feeding tube, Sir?"

"Yes."

"Well, we can exchange that. Instead of putting it through his mouth, we can put an incision directly into his stomach instead. It's a small operation, and the wound will be covered with a bandage. We can then feed him directly, and his face will be clear of the feeding tube."

"Whatever you can do Doctor, to keep Adam alive while we await God's will."

"Yes, as I say, the hospital management will be in touch. I'm purely a health professional."

"Why do you keep saying that?"

Dad, stay calm.

"Sorry Mr Pound, saying what?"

"Hospital management, in touch and that. He's my boy. I get to decide about him. God bless my wife, Valerie, she gave birth to him, pure and without sin."

"It is not my place to say."

"And then some terrorist comes along and blows him up. My innocent boy. And those terrorists, they failed didn't they. And now you, and your medical conspiracy here, you want to put him to death when he is still a living, breathing, child of God. We've only just found him. Found ourselves. I will not allow it."

"Mr Pound, I must ask you to calm down."

Dad. Angry dad. Full of the fury of the Old Testament.

"Go on, Doctor. Away with you. I'm going to take my son out of here. Away from your interfering hands. God has a plan for my boy. You don't get to decide."

"Sir, I shall be noting this conversation in our harassment protocol."

"Go on then, quick as you can. Run along, Doctor Atwan. And you, Nurse."

Door.

Don't leave me alone with him. Please Doctor.

"Now you. Adam! We start again. Our Father in heaven..."

Never. I will never pray with you. You cannot hurt me any more. Where is Dillon? Without him, I don't want to be alive. Bring back my gentle man.

22

Door.

"DI Ling, could you take a recorded note of those present please."

"Yes, Ma'am. For the record we have myself, DI Ling, Metropolitan Police; DCI Pierce, Metropolitan Police; Ms Doctor Atwan, general consultant at St Michael's Hospital; Ms Ikana Okereke, Senior Social Worker, London Borough of Lambeth, and Mr Dillon Kendrick, London Borough of Westminster social services volunteer responsible adult."

Dillon? Is that you? You're back. I thought you were gone. I thought I would die. Oh, thank God.

"All present and correct?" *It was DCI Pierce.*

"If I may?" *It was Dillon.*

So good to hear your voice.

"Go ahead."

"You forgot David. I mean, Adam here."

"Of course. Apologies, Adam Pound, patient at St Michael's Hospital. Doctor Atwan, can you confirm that Mr Pound is not currently able to communicate with us?"

Dillon, you're back!

"That is correct, Detective Inspector Ling."

"Okay, well, thank you to all present. We've been advised by our own legal team that this discussion should take place in the presence of Mr Adam Pound and his advocates, even though he is not currently capable of communicating. Should he become fully conscious, according to our legal team, he might otherwise have redress against us for not fully understanding and communicating his needs. Is that everyone's understanding?"

"Yes, though I remain in doubt Mr Pound will ever be in any state to understand, and definitely not to communicate." *It was Doctor Atwan.*

"Nevertheless, it is my legal understanding we should proceed in this manner. And this is also why we have invited Mr Kendrick into the room again, as a responsible adult who is able to ensure Mr Pound's interests are protected."

I thought Dad had thrown you out? You've come back for me.

"So, as we have come to understand, this is becoming a further complicated matter outside the scope of the investigations into the bombing, which is why my colleague DI Ling is here, and Ms Okereke from Lambeth. I'm passing this entirely separate aspect of Mr Pound's case to DI Ling, who will take it from here."

What's going on, Dillon? I'm so glad you're back.

"If you will, DI Ling?"

"Thank you Ma'am. The Met was approached by Wandsworth social services two days ago, when the real name of Adam Pound was released to the media. The family are known to social services there, and there is some doubt as to whether the parents, a Mr Geoff and Mrs Valerie Pound, should be in position to make decisions on their son's behalf."

"Ms Okereke, do you have anything to add?" *It was DCI Pierce.*

"Thank you. The Pound family have long been in reluctant contact with Lambeth, regarding child protection. There have been, in the past, concerns expressed by neighbours, as well as schools, about the welfare of their children.

"I believe, according to our records, there are six. Four boys, and two girls. Now all over 18, and out of our jurisdiction. But when they were under 18, engagement with our services was very poor."

"Were there any cases?" *It was DI Ling.*

"No, no actual removals or official reports took place. But in the past we have reached out to the family to offer extra support, which has always been rejected.

"However, there have been a number of suspect hospital admissions which naturally were reported to us. I and former colleagues met with doctors a number of times over a number of years, with regards to suspect injuries. We were unable to pin anything down. Through the schools, we also attempted to carry out mental health assessments of the children, but attendance was always low and inconsistent. May I be frank?"

"Please, go ahead." *It was DCI Pierce.*

"Thank you." *It was Ms Okereke.*

"The Pound family are evangelical Christians, and are believed to be part of a group that one might regard as particularly strict, enclosed, almost cult-like. I am a Christian myself, but their beliefs are extreme. Which of course is not our business, but some of their practices are considered controversial."

"Can you clarify, please?" *It was DI Ling.*

"Adults consent to verbal and we suspect physical punishment, in order to atone for their sins. Members are required to declare everything about themselves to the congregation and ask for forgiveness if they are considered to have done wrong. Children are told their school religious education, sex education, and personal and social education is wrong, the work of the devil, and are required to reject it as a sin, publicly in front of all the congregation."

"That sounds like child abuse." *It was Dillon.*

"Now, let's be careful with our choice of words here please." *It was DI Ling.*

"Sorry."

"There are some specific concerns about the church, that is for sure. But it is very hard to generalise. Family membership is certainly flagged up on our system, but we have to prove actual malpractice or unreasonable behaviour in every case. Being a church member doesn't mean anything, though we have prosecuted some parents for keeping their children from school. Most other things, we've not been able to make stick." *It was Ms Okereke.*

"So, where does Adam Pound come in to all of this? His parents are obnoxious, so what? The father has certainly been rude to me." *It was Doctor Atwan.*

Too right. Crazy. Hateful.

"I'm not sure if I need to inform you that this particular church is not sympathetic in the slightest to the gay community. It is considered a sin to be gay, and they are quite open about running gay conversion therapies." *It was DI Ling.*

"I thought those therapies had been banned?" *It was Dillon.*

"I've investigated. They're on the books for consultation, but currently it's allowed."

"That's right. Even those from outside the church can pay for a programme for a youth, or whatever, to go through the so called treatment." *It was Ms Okereke.*

"That particular therapy is of concern to us. Children who have spoken up about their feelings are punished as sinful. Made to recant those feelings. To call themselves sinners. Again and again and again."

"How do you know all this?" *It was Dillon.*

"There are some 'escapees' from the church. They'd gone in for the community aspect, but found themselves in a cult." *It was Ms Okereke.*

"Again, let's be careful with our language, please." *It was DI Ling.*

"Sorry, Inspector. This church certainly advocates gay conversion therapy, and it involves self-flagellation, enforced silence, being locked in rooms for days, and being forced to continuously pray. And in the most extreme cases, at least as far as the witnesses claim, though we've never been able to prove it, those undergoing the conversion are expected to carry out some of the punishments that Jesus underwent."

I know those punishments, Dillon. God knows, I know those punishments.

"Go ahead, Ms Okereke." *It was DI Ling.*

"Well, the wearing of a crown of thorns. Washing their feet with very hot water, to clear away their sins. Forty days of starvation. Who knows, just look in the Bible."

"Okay, that's enough. I think you've made yourself clear. Please get to your main point, Ms Okereke." *It was DCI Pierce.*

"We would like to contend, as we attempted to with some of the other Pound children some years ago, that Adam here is not safe to be under the care of his parents. Particularly as he attended the Pride Festival."

"Oh my God." *It was Dillon.*

Don't worry Dillon, they can't get to me now.

"Mr Pound is not a child, but we would argue that in his

current situation, he cannot speak or make decisions for himself. We intend to make a temporary order of court, which we hope to submit this afternoon. If granted, we should be able to take over Adam's responsibility for a week - no more - while further investigations take place. If we find grounds, only then could we call for a more permanent order. The courts can also demand a media blackout, and I suggest we push for that."

"Thank you, Ms Okereke." *It was DI Ling.*

"This is a vulnerable person issue, and Ms Okereke will be pursuing that end of things. Meantime, I have been asked by DCI Pierce to investigate the Pound family further, including their church. I believe DCI Pierce has been given unique grounds for me to do that."

"Thank you, DI Ling. Yes, there is something I now need to share, but it is vital that it does not leave this room, as it may need to be used in evidence. I'm assuming absolute confidence, because it may be vital to our investigations into the bombing too." *It was DCI Pierce.*

"Yes." *It was Ms Okereke.*

"Yes, of course." *It was Dillon.*

"Yes, go ahead." *It was Doctor Atwan.*

"Forensics have found a single foot, as they have been sifting through their remaining evidence from the bombing at Piccadilly Circus. It is a male, left foot, of around size 10. My understanding is it was blown out of the main parade, when the bomb went off, and was assumed very badly burned.

"However, on closer inspection, forensics found the foot suffered only superficial burning. Genetic matching shows the foot belongs to Adam Pound, and on the foot - all around it - there is clear evidence of scalding."

Door.

"Adam."

Oh, my God, it's you. Please call me David, I'm not Adam any more.

"The doctor and the police are coming over this morning, but I thought I'd be back early to give you a brief. They always talk over you."

Yes, but you don't Dillon. I'm so glad you're back.

"So, it looks like you and me have a little more time together. Because, well, it looks like - for the time being - social services have got a temporary ban on your parents making decisions for you. I don't know the full details. I think the media are banned from talking about it too.

"I don't know how long this is going to last, but I hope it's not too complex and ugly for you. The whole thing, Adam, it's challenging for me. I can tell you that."

Don't worry, I'm here, with you.

"Well, anyway, I'll continue my job. Looking after your interests. Oh, Adam, I do wish I knew what you wanted. It's hard being an advocate if, well, I don't know what your preferences are."

Dillon, I think I want to be with you.

"So, I brought a paper. Like last time. News of the bombing has died down now. Guess the Foreign Office wanted it done and dusted so the Saudis didn't get too serious. Looks like they're going to be friends again.

"But this new thing about Noor Hisham not being the bomber. That's thrown everything into question again. The police are standing firm. The government is raging."

Door.

"Ah, Doctor Atwan. DI Ling."

"Mr Kendrick. This is Jo Lacey, from our forensic investigation team. She's been doing a lot of the examination of body parts recovered from the bombing. She was the one who identified scalding on the left foot, the one that turned out to be from Adam here." *It was DI Ling.*

"Can you explain, Ms Lacey?" *It was Dillon.*

"Sure. Each of the body parts has to be photographed and, if you don't mind the language, fitted with the original body so that burials, and cremations can be carried out. It also helps us map where the explosion came from. Say, a torso has shrapnel impact on the left hand side, it's clear that the bomb exploded in that direction.

"We use computer imaging and matching, along with DNA sampling, to build a picture of the explosion, and of those caught up in it. Where they were, how close to the explosion, how it affected the crowd. Some of our modelling helped the police to identify that the bombing couldn't have come from any rucksack hidden on Noor Husain's back. She was hit on the front. And that matches the footage of her carrying a rucksack in her hand, not wearing one.

"So we also look at the types of injury. In this case, it's been mainly burns, shrapnel from nails and bolts, and in rarer cases some glass blown out from windows.

"The left foot that we found, which we matched to Adam Pound by DNA, was burned on the right side. From just above the ankle, right down and across to the front of the foot."

Shuffling.

"Do you mind if I show you? I have some photographs."

"That would be useful." *It was Doctor Atwan.*

"Okay, evidence of burning from the explosion and heat all along this area. There's clearly some melting of whatever plastic based shoe he was wearing, I think we can assume a trainer of some kind. We could track down the brand, but it's not a priority.

"But on the left side of his foot, I guess the one facing away from the blast, well, there remained some trainer and even sock, despite the fact that Adam's foot was entirely dismembered.

"Once the foot had been identified, we took away those parts, but underneath found further evidence of burning. But this was much older, and scalding rather than dry heat. It raised interest in the lab, so we proceeded to the right of the foot again, and picked away some of the plastic and dry heat burning from the right side, and underneath, we found the same scalding."

"Can you sum up?" *It was DI Ling.*

"Sorry, yes, Adam's left foot was very badly scalded. Our estimate would be that the injury could have been ten years old. Maybe more."

"Now, Geoff Pound claims, Adam's dad, was a - let me find my notes - yes, a stupid boy, who dropped a kettle of water on his feet when he was a kid." *It was DI Ling.*

Don't call him Dad. He's not my Dad. Not any more.

"The thing is, these scars show sustained injury. Not a one-off incident. Layers of scarring."

"What does that mean?" *It was Doctor Atwan.*

"It means that Adam must have dropped that kettle a number of times. Waited for his feet to heal, then dropped it again. At least twice." *It was Ms Lacey.*

"Best, and most obvious guess, after speaking to Wandsworth, is that Adam underwent some kind of punishment as a child, or at least in his teens." *It was DI Ling.*

"Who would pour boiling water onto a child's feet?" *It was Dillon.*

"Who indeed?" *It was DI Ling.*

It doesn't matter, as long as you're here. Dad learned the hard way. His father did it to him, for drinking and pinching church property. He did it to me for being gay.

"So, we're here today to do something quite difficult." *It was Doctor Atwan.*

"We need to examine David and look at the injuries sustained in the bombing, but also look for anything further. Deeper, as it were. Injuries sustained before the bombing, even back to his teens.

"Mr Kendrick, given that Adam here is unable to give his consent, and his parents are currently considered incapable, we need to ask you to observe and give consent on behalf of Westminster social services."

Yes, Dillon. Show them what Dad did to me.

"Of course, whatever you need to do, as long as we maintain his dignity and privacy?"

"All agreed? Okay, let's proceed." *It was DI Ling.*

Silence.

"What are we going to do?" *It was Dillon.*

"We'll check him from head to toe, er upper legs." *It was Ms Lacey.*

"May I? Here we see burned hair, but it is beginning to grow back again. Heavy scarring, from the emergency brain surgery."

"We had to remove some large pieces of skull from his brain. There are poor neurological pathways. It is why he has no consciousness. Our estimate is when the bomb exploded, he hit the pavement head first. He came in with this wound stuffed with a Pride flag." *It was Doctor Atwan.*

"Okay, so that's internal injuries at the head. Externally, at the head, we have some facial scaring, but again, clearly part of the incident. We have some photos of Adam before the bomb, from his parents.

"Apart from the clear injures we can see from the bomb, everything looks as it was then. Neck and chest. Shoulders. It looks good to me. Some singeing of hairs, and some mild shrapnel injuries. I suspect his T-shirt burned away from him, saving his skin. I see that a lot."

If only you could really see. If only.

"Chest. Only shrapnel from the bomb. Stomach. Nothing to speak off. Can we turn him over?"

"I'll help." *It was Dillon.*

"Thank you." *It was Dr Atwan.*

Are you touching me, Dillon? Where are you touching me?

"Okay, looking at Adam's shoulders again. It looks like he took the bulk of the explosion from the front, there's nothing to see here. Upper back and shoulders, pretty sound."

Find it, Dillon. Find it.

"Lower back. The famous diamond of moles." *It was Doctor Atwan.*

"Sorry?" *It was Ms Lacey.*

"No, carry on. There's a diamond of moles on his right hand side, on his back. It's how we identified him as Adam Pound."

"Ah, I see. Okay, if we move lower. Wait, here."

"Bed creases?" *It was DI Ling.*

"No. The orderlies have been moving him too frequently to develop bed sores." *It was Doctor Atwan.*

"And see, if you press them, they remain red. They don't go white. These are scars." *It was Ms Lacey.*

"Oh." *It was Dillon.*

"And see how they cross, straight lines but crossing? Three, or maybe four of them? Very faint."

"Or are we imagining it?" *It was DI Ling.*

"Well, theoretically they could have come from the

bomb. His belt, perhaps, friction burning him. But the actual scarring, though certainly not very clear, I'd argue goes deep under the skin."

"What are your suspicions, Ms Lacey?"

"Some sort of tying? Or straps?"

"Could it be bondage? Like being tied down?" *It was Doctor Atwan.*

"I'd have to investigate further. But this looks more like, well, like burning."

"Scalding again?" *It was Dillon.*

"No, possibly friction?"

"Wait. Excuse me, Mr Kendrick, but do you feel it appropriate to go further down? Onto his buttocks?" *It was DI Ling.*

"If you're thinking what I'm thinking?" *It was Dillon.*

Oh, Dillon, are you thinking what I'm thinking? Are you going to see my bum? I hope it doesn't look too bad to you.

"Okay, and here we go. They're faint, but I think if you'd like to get closer?"

Minor grumbling.

"Ms Lacey?"

"Its whipping, isn't it? With a leather strap? A belt? Not recent. Not recent at all. The skin has recovered, grown over the original injuries. Look, it's all stretched out. Flattened as the skin has grown. As the man has grown."

"Ms Lacey, can you state it for the record?" *It was DI Ling.*

"Yes, Detective Inspector, we are strongly suspecting Adam Pound was whipped in his younger years. Maybe..."

Ten years. It was ten years ago. And for five years before that.

"Ten years ago, even more. At the time when he was a child. The injuries are not fresh, so we can assume some kind of child abuse by today's standards. Even ten year's ago standards."

"Whipping?" *It was Dillon.*

Lashes, Dillon. Dad called them lashes. Proverbs 20. 'Lashes and wounds purge away evil, and beatings cleanse the innermost parts.'

"So, what do we do now?" *It was Doctor Atwan.*

"I think we have grounds to extend Adam's care under the state, that's for sure. We'll need to be careful about accusations, but we could ask the court for more time." *It was DI Ling.*

"To do what?" *It was Dillon.*

"Look for more evidence of child abuse. Investigate the family further. Perhaps the church? Bring the Pounds in for questioning?"

"Couldn't you X-ray David?" *It was Dillon.*

Oh, you're so smart, Dillon.

"That is a great idea. The CAT scans when he came in looked at his brain and internal organs. If we did a full body X-ray, we could get a better picture of any older injuries. Thank you, Mr Kendrick."

"Please, call me Dillon."

Please Dillon, call me boyfriend.

23

Noise.

In the corridor outside.

Not just the normal hospital noise.

Beep. Ah. Beep. Ah. Beep. Ah.

Trolleys shifting.

Shouting. Banging.

"Let me in."

Bang, bang, bang.

Doors rattling.

"Sir, I have to ask you..."

A woman's voice.

"Get out of my way."

Bang, bang, bang.

"Let me see my son."

Oh, God, it was Dad.

Door. Rattle.

Don't let him in. Oh, please. He's drunk. You don't know him when he's drunk. Protect me.

"Sir, Mr Pound, please stand away. I shall call the police."

A woman's voice again.

"Open these bloody doors. Give me that card, I'll open them myself."

"Sir, I've notified security."

"Good, they can let me in."

Bang, bang, bang.

"Sir, the patients!"

"Screw the patients. I want to see my son. I have a right."

"Ah security, we have an A1 issue, Ward 414."

Crunching sound. "Make... self safe. Do not approach..."

"Sir, I'm locking myself in my office. Security are on their way. You must stop this behaviour. You are on CCTV."

Door slam.

Heavy footsteps.

"We're hospital security. Sir, we are recording."

"Let me in to see my son?"

"Sir, have you been drinking?"

"Let me in."

Bang, bang, bang.

Crunch.

"Request police backup."

"Sir, we are asking you to calm down."

"But my son,"

Dad. Shouting.

"Sir, it will look far better for you if you are calm when the police arrive. They take threats to patients and staff very seriously." *It was a guard.*

"Good, I want them to see what they're doing to me. To my wife! We have a right."

"Sir, you will have to talk to the authorities about that. I don't know your situation."

"We're trying to get our son back."

Calmer now. Oh, Dad. Don't fret. Please, let me go. Get on with your life.

"They've taken him away. They want him to die here. That's why they've taken him."

"Sir, please take a seat. We can bring you some black coffee." *It was a guard.*

Dad, please, let me be free.

"Okay, okay. I suppose you better take me in."

"Sir, we're security guards. You've caused a disturbance, and now I can see that you're calm. If you're able to wait a few more minutes, we can clear things with the police. We have CCTV and chest mounted cameras, I think they'll look on your actions sympathetically."

"If they knew. If they knew they've taken Adam away from us? They should be arresting the doctors. And social services."

"Sir, I'm sure the police will just ask you to leave the hospital. We have people with... alcohol problems here, all the time."

"I don't have a problem. Adam is my son. A child of Christ."

"But you have been drinking?"

"Are you not sinful officers?"

"Sorry, Sir, we're security guards."

"You are good men. I can see that. Have you heard the word of the Lord."

"Sir, take a seat."

Door. Heavy boots.

"Stand aside."

"It's okay, officer. I think this man has calmed down. Isn't that right, Mr...?"

"Pound, it's Geoff Pound?"

Dad? Are you crying, Dad?

Crunch.

"Three, one, two."

Crunch.

"Go ahead, officer."

Crunch.

"Okay, we have a drunk and disorderly, floor four of St Michael's hospital. Two officers on location, hospital security also. Call off back-up. I think we can handle this one."

Crunch.

"Roger that."

"Okay, Mr Pound. Take a seat. Shall we ask the nurse to join us? And we can all talk about what happened here."

Quiet.

Click.

"Nurse, come out, it's safe."

"This is Mr Pound. His son is in a bay, further up the corridor. But we're under instructions that he's not to be allowed in. It's a vulnerable person issue, officer." *A female voice.*

"Understood, Nurse. Thank you. Mr Pound, is this correct? You are not allowed to visit your son?" *It was a male voice.*

"Yes, officer. But it's not fair. We're taking it to court."

"That is as may be, Sir. But as I understand it, you are currently not entitled to be here. I'm going to ask you to leave. Have you been drinking, Sir?"

Silence.

"Okay, then I'm going to presume you have. And that you couldn't possibly have driven here?"

Silence.

"Good, then. PC Raymond, I think we can give Mr Pound here a lift home, can't we. That'll settle the matter?" *It was the man again.*

"Thank you. And, well, sorry Nurse. Really sorry. I didn't mean to scare you. Officer, can you drop me at the top of my street. I'm ashamed. I don't want Valerie to see me like this."
It was Dad.

"We'll accompany you out, Sir."

Silence.

Oh Dad. I just don't know how to feel about you. You sad, sad man.

"This is the place?"

"Yep, just there."

I don't know that voice.

Wmmm... Wmmm.... Wmmmmmmm

Oh God, no. Not the drill.

Click.

Wmmm... Wmmm.... Wmmmmmmm

Wmmm... Wmmm.... Wmmmmmmm

Oh Pastor, what are you doing to me now? Not the drill again. Please, I can't stand to listen to it. What are you doing to me?

Wmmm... Wmmm.... Wmmmmmmm

What, what's going on?

Click. Clunk.

Scraaaape.

Oh, no. Let me wake up from this. Please, no more memories.

"Jesus Christ, this one's a stubborn one. If I can just..."

Wmmm... Wmmm....

"That's it. Now, if you can just hand me those screws?"

Oh my God! No Pastor.

Whirr... Whirr...

24

Door.

"Sergeant, please stay at this door. We are not to be disturbed." *It was DI Ling.*

"Yes, Ma'am."

"Doctor, in the presence of Mr Kendrick, and Adam Pound, can you please repeat what you just told me."

"Mr Pound chose to pay a little visit last night. Banging on doors. Waking and distressing other patients. Demanding to be let in to see his son."

"The police were called?" *It was Dillon.*

"Yes, security say the officers logged the incident and asked for the CCTV and chest footage to be stored, in case it was needed. They took him home. I've had quite enough of that man. I'll be pleased if Mr Pound is never allowed back in here."

"Sounds pretty desperate?" *It was DI Ling.*

"I'm not surprised. Who knows what he would have done if he'd got in. Our night shift nurse and security acted well, in the circumstances."

"Meaning?"

"It could have been a lot worse. We've had the results back from the X-rays."

"Continue, please Doctor. I'm taking notes." *It was DI Ling.*

"Thanks, the X-rays show some cracking in Adam's thigh bones, both sides. Not breaks, but splinters. His wrists, both of them, also show signs of distress. On the right, in particular, there has been a fracture, we can estimate from about fifteen years ago."

"In your experience, Doctor?" *It was DI Ling.*

"I'm not a paediatric expert, but I'd strongly suggest shaking, squeezing, twisting of limbs, maybe even handcuffing?"

Oh, my God.

"Given what we've seen, could you see this, perhaps, as the result of - when Adam was younger - I don't know how to say it, some kind of body manipulation. Physical twisting, Doctor?" *It was DI Ling.*

It was a long time ago. He can't hurt me any more.

"Definitely not my field, Inspector. We'd need an expert to look at that. I won't say, one way or another on the record."

"But they would be childhood injuries?"

"Yes, Inspector."

"Grounds to keep Adam away from his parents?"

"Again, not my place to say, sorry. I'm just interested in his health now, not his past. But I can get a paeds expert to look at the X-rays, and make a statement." *It was Doctor Atwan.*

"Thank you Doctor. I'll consult with social services. I think it will need to be Westminster who'll need to make the case for an extension. That means it'll likely be you, Mr

Kendrick, if the extension is granted. You happy enough with that." *It was DI Ling.*

Silence.

Dillon?

"Mr Kendrick?"

"Yes, yes, sorry. Of course. I know the situation best. It's been tough so far, might as well see it through. No wonder Mr Pound wanted me out of the way. I guess I'm Adam's only voice. And I'm hurting real bad for him."

Don't worry, Dillon. I'm safe now.

"I'm sorry, Mr Kendrick. At least Adam doesn't know or feel anything." *It was Doctor Atwan.*

"Are you sure, Doctor? I mean, it would be awful if he could hear us after all this time. I talk to him, you know, to reassure him. Maybe to reassure myself. But, what a horror?"

"Mr Kendrick, Dillon, Adam is long gone. He's not suffering from his injuries, and he's not suffering anymore from what someone did to him."

You're wrong, Doctor. I hurt. I suffer, every day, I suffer. I suffer because I can remember.

Not the bomb.

Not the explosion.

But I remember Dad. And the church. And the pastor. And the programme.

I am not gay. I am not gay.

I repeated it. I had to go back to the programme three times. Three times repent. Three times, for the lashes. Three times for the cleansing. Three times to have my wrists tied behind my back.

I am not gay. I am not gay.

It didn't work. I am gay. I think I love you, Dillon. It hurts, but I do. And I feel sick. Sick with myself. Sick of being gay.

God created me, yet God punishes me. That I don't understand.

"Thank you, Doctor. I'll try to take that on board."

Don't go, Dillon.

Silence.

Dillon?

Door.

Dillon, is it you?

"Knock, knock."

Oh, Dillon it is you.

"I've brought someone to see you. I hope you don't mind. I thought it the kindest thing to do?"

"Hello."

Wait, I know that voice. From the TV.

"Can he hear me?"

"We like to imagine he does. Better that, than to talk over him, isn't that right Adam?"

"Okay."

I can't place you. How do I know you? Talk some more.

"Well, firstly, I wanted to say how sorry I am that you have ended up in this state. It was a cruel, harsh thing..."

What is that Dillon? Is he crying.

"It's okay, Mr Brookes. I know how hard this is for you. You've been through a lot. Here, let me get you some tissues from his cupboard."

Brookes?

"Sorry, it's just..."

"I understand. In your own time. We're not going anywhere."

You're so caring, Dillon.

"Thanks, Mr Kendrick."

"Dillon, please."

"You should call me Peter."

"Peter then. It's okay. Those aren't the first tears shed in this room, I can tell you."

"It was just so hard."

"I know."

"Okay, Adam. I'm so sorry this happened to you. My daughter, Charlotte, she was also killed by the bombing. I mean, not also, but... Well, killed. Anyway, I wanted to say sorry. From my family to yours. My daughter, she didn't plant the bomb. Everyone knows that now. But I need you, and you Mr Kendrick, Dillon, to know: my daughter was good and sweet. She was a princess. She was quiet and easily led. I am to blame for that. I never gave her the attention she needed. I let her down..."

"It's okay, it's not your fault Peter. Take your time."

"She was easily led. I thought it was just being a teenager. But I suppose that doesn't matter now. But Adam, I'm proud of my daughter. Maybe she didn't know what she was, or who she was, and I could have done more to help her. Been a safety net. If only, if only there had been some, I don't know, intervention."

I understand. All I wanted was a safety net, too. But no-one ever caught me. You are ten times the father mine was.

"Anyway, I wanted to see you. To express my sympathy."

"Thank you, Mr Brookes. I can assure you Adam would extend the same to you. I really am sorry for your loss."

"Ah, well, you know Mr Kendrick. This whole thing: it makes you question the world. Whether anything really matters. Just animals on a planet, after all. Think about it: it doesn't matter who's to blame. Who got hurt. Whether the Saudis buy their weapons from the UK. I mean, it really doesn't. Might as well just trudge along in our own shit."

"I'm sorry you see it that way, Mr Brookes."

"No, really. I'm over it. Nothing matters. But thanks for seeing me anyway. I wish you both the best."

"Let me see you out."

Door.

Dillon?

"I'm still here, David. He's given up. I understand. But I've not given up."

He's right. There's nothing to look forward to with me. I'm finished.

"Whoa, Squirrel, here he is."

"Ad, that you boy?"

"Looks better than last time."

Dillon? Who are these people? Dillon, are you there?

"Check the door, mate and stand guard. Can you lock the door?"

"It doesn't lock."

"Okay, put your foot in front of it. Don't let anyone in, got it?"

Who are you?

"Right, chap, Ad. Adam. We've been mates for a long time, yeah. Like, a real long time? There's things we've always done, yeah, you know to protect each other."

"Yeah, like that time when you told Lamo's mum he was over at your house, when he was really over getting to second base with Selina Gerard."

"Shut up, Squirrel, this is serious."

Squirrel? Lamo? I don't know you people. You've got the wrong guy.

"Listen, Ad. They're sniffing around. The cops. And the Mussies, they're getting itchy. The police say that white girl turned Muslim didn't do the bomb. So we're just saying."

"Just saying."

"Shut up, Squirrel."

"So we're just saying, should you, well, come awake or whatever, you don't know us. Me, and Squirrel, and, well, Blue Team."

"Tell him, Lamo."

"Shut it, Squirrel. Listen, Ad, that bomb. Piccadilly Circus. We had nothing to do with it, understand? I mean, there are secrets and there are secrets. But we wouldn't do that. Jesus, we wouldn't lad. Just so you know. And that, well, if you wake up, all that was just talk - you know in the pub that time - just talk mate. I was five pints to the wind. So were you."

"It was just talk, Ad."

"Squirrel, next time you speak, I'll knock your block off."

"Sorry, Lamo."

"Ad, listen. It was just talk, wasn't it? Just pub talk. Just so you know, Ad. In case you, well, come alive or whatever. Just talk. Or, maybe, don't even mention it. Blue Team, we don't exist any more. Never did."

"Tell him, Lamo."

"Ad."

"Tell him."

"Fucks sake, Squirrel, I'm doing it. Ad, sorry to have to say it, but well, you know, loose lips and that. There were only the three of us there, at the pub. It was just talk. So, don't break the chain, it's all we're saying."

"We'll break your fucking arms as well as your legs if you do."

"I'll break *your* arms, if you don't shut it, Squirrel. Come on, let's get out of here."

"Blue Team."

Door.

Slam.

What the hell just happened? Dillon, are you there? Dillon? Please, help me, Dillon.

25

Door.

"DCI Pierce, good to see you."

"And you, Mr Kendrick. Doctor Atwan too. I'm here to update you both, and Adam."

"On what?" *It was Dillon.*

"On our investigations into his family, Mr Kendrick. After the fuss the other night, we wanted to get right onto this. We've had approval to arrest Mr Pound on suspicion of child abuse, of Adam here, and possibly of other youngsters in and around his church."

"Oh, my God." *It was Doctor Atwan.*

"Yes, they would let anyone run the Sunday school club back in the day, it seems. Obviously, nothing is proven. But we have him in for questioning."

What about Mum. Where's Mum?

"So, you've arrested Adam's dad?" *It was Dillon.*

"We're questioning him at Victoria. So, well, I wanted to let you know out of courtesy. But also, is there anything else at all? Anything you've noticed, Mr Kendrick, about Adam. Anything we should be questioning Mr Pound about?"

"I can't think of anything. He threw me out, every time he came."

That's right. Just like he would throw others out of the room, before the pastor came. Before he began his lessons.

"Okay, I understand. But if anything occurs? And you too, Doctor."

"And the wife?" *It was Doctor Atwan.*

Sweet, sweet Doctor Atwan. I used to think you were cold. Now I can see you're just angry.

"Mrs Pound is with neighbours. We have no reason right now to suspect any criminal behaviour. She could be a witness, even a victim. We're looking after her, just now."

"Do you think I should reach out to her?"

"I don't think so, Mr Kendrick. It might muddy the waters even further. We can only hold Mr Pound for two nights at most."

"Oh." *It was the doctor.*

"Don't worry, as long as Wandsworth hold their line, their burden of proof is far less than mine. He won't be able to get in to see David. But if we can't press charges, or even if we can and the magistrate sees Geoff Pound as no longer a threat to society, he'll be released pending prosecution. That could take many months, or if this is purely a historical case, many years. Crown Prosecution might not decide to pursue at all. All in the public interest, of course."

"Okay." *It was Doctor Atwan.*

"You wouldn't believe, Doctor, how many cases we can't prosecute because the CPS won't carry it forward. Cases much clearer than this, I can tell you."

Silence.

"Thank you for your time, DCI Pierce." *It was Dillon.*

Always Dillon. I'm sorry I'm such a burden to you.

"Well, good luck. With the media etcetera, Mr Kendrick.

You might need some back up from social services. Media relations and things?"

"I'll call my oversight team."

"All good then. Well, I suppose I better get on."

"You look tired?" *It was Doctor Atwan.*

"Really?" *It was DCI Pierce.*

Silence.

"I suppose so, it's the juggling. I'm getting a lot of pressure from the Home Office, to get the bombing pinned down. I know he's briefing against my boss, trying to say we failed by naming Noor Hisham early. But we always said investigations were ongoing. Now he's braying for another name, but police work just doesn't go that quickly.

"Then there's the Pride Bomb Justice Campaign. They want to know why we didn't prevent the bomb and what compensation we're going to provide for families. And the likes of Geoff Pound, and there are loads of them, wanting to know - 'in this era of extremism' - why we let the Pride Festival happen at all? Ah, the irony there.

"And anyway, it's not our choice. We're just the police. It's the government that allows protests, so we get back to the Home Office again. We're always caught in the middle. We don't get everything right, but we do the very best we can."

"I'm sure you do, and that scenario is certainly familiar to me." *It was Doctor Atwan.*

"Sorry. Yes. Dropped my guard a bit there. Back to business. Thank you all so very much for what you're doing, Dillon. I mean, with Adam. It must be, well, very unrewarding."

"Actually, Inspector, it's the most challenging, but also the most rewarding thing I've ever done.

Oh, Dillon. You are so kind. I'm going to call you boyfriend.

"Hey, we're not supposed to get on so well. You know -

police and responsible adults - those are the unwritten rules." *It was DCI Pierce.*

"When we see good work done, it should be acknowledged. On both sides. So thank you."

"Okay, enough. Back to it then." *It was DCI Pierce.*

"Here, I brought you the paper."

Dillon?

"Just the usual I'm afraid. Superstar David all over the front page. I'll give you the headlines. Let me see."

"Okay, here we go. Your dad has been arrested, that much we know. Though the papers can't say what for - court of protection restrictions in this kind of case, I think - so the paper is saying, 'suspected crimes in the past'.

They're loving that it's *your* dad, though. National hero and all that. Another chance to put your face on the front. Just a little one of your dad, all dressed up for church. Shame they're still using that one of you here in this hospital. I'm sure your folks gave them some much better ones."

"So, let me see, 'Mr Pound's solicitor is expected to make a statement today, but has already said his client denies any wrong doing.' Looks like he's given a no-comment interview to the police, that's what the lawyers always say when they've got no idea what's going on.

"And, sorry, here we go, 'The arrest of Mr Pound and the situation of his son Adam Pound, who remains in a coma after the Piccadilly bombing on 21st June, are not thought to be connected.'

"Looks like the police don't have much, Adam. Or nothing solid. I guess there's no proof linking him directly to your injuries. It's all circumstantial. Obvious as daylight to us, Adam, but there's a difference between obvious and proof.

"At least the court of protection can cast a wider net, that's my experience anyway. Your dad only has to have done that to you, on the balance of probabilities. There's no need for absolute proof. Many don't seem to know that."

He did it, Dillon. I remember. The pain.

"Well, at least that's better for you. You'll not have him around again, unless the court of protection rules in their favour. Your dad might not even put up a fight."

Oh, he will Dillon. You don't know my Dad. It's his God-given right to take me under his responsibility. You don't know how that man thinks.

"Oh, here's another column, Adam. Do you want me to read it to you? It's an opinion piece, Rachel Jones. I quite like her stuff. Seems pretty reasonable. Let me see...

"Oh, here: *'The name of the Piccadilly Bomber might not be known, but there is one person's life the explosion continues to affect. And not in a good way. That of Adam Pound. It is time to allow that poor man, bereft of any senses or any understanding of his life gone or in the present, a dignified death. Whether the Metropolitan Police identify the bomber or not, Adam should be allowed to pass away without any outside influence.'*

"Wow, what do you think?"

Silence.

"God, I wish you could answer. I wish I knew what you thought. Is she right, Adam? I'm supposed to be removed, but I'm human."

You're the best, Dillon.

"I can't stand the idea of you passing away, it would feel like losing you. I'm not supposed to get emotionally involved, but whatever. I want what's best for you? My real view? I wish they'd just allow you to go in peace, Adam.

"I don't understand the politics. Everyone has strong opinions. Jesus, you should look on Twitter. But being here with you? I just want it to end. I know you're not suffering, at least not in that way. But after our deaths, we live though our memories, don't we? Shouldn't people's memories of you be good ones? Not, 'the man who was stuck in hospital for years', but the man who dies, peacefully, proud of who he is, among his own people?"

You're so right, Dillon.

"And now I'm babbling. Everyone else seems so certain. I've got no clue. God, let me see if I can find some whales or dolphins in this bloody paper."

Are you crying Dillon?

"Sorry, Adam. Stupid of me. There's a lot of pressure, you know."

Oh, Dillon. How can I reach for you?

"Sorry. Got to pull myself together. Maybe I shouldn't be here with you. Maybe I need to pass you on to someone else. I need to get back to my life."

No, Dillon. Don't pass me on. That's what everyone is doing. I'm not an object. I'm not a news story. I'm not a pawn.

Dillon. Dillon, are you there?

Silence.

Dillon?

"I'll see you tomorrow."

26

Knock.

Door.

Why do they always knock? Just come in, for God's sake.

"Adam, good morning. It's Detective Chief Inspector Pierce, with DI Ling. And this is..."

"Hello."

A man's voice? Strange accent.

"Well, we'll see who this is. Carey Armstrong, do you recognise this man?"

"Yes, definitely. We were at the Two Brewers together, close to Clapham, the day before the bombing. We met at the bar."

"Are you sure about that, Mr Armstrong? Do you know his name?"

"I recognise him from the paper. Only better now, his wounds have obviously cleared up."

Hello? I know your voice. Are you American?

"And you spent time with him?"

"Yes, we had a few drinks. And we talked about the

United States, that's where I'm from. He said he wanted to go there."

Yes, American. San Fransisco. I remember.

"But, no. He didn't tell me his name that night. I only know it from the paper. It was a, well, a chance meeting. I'm in on some long term business from the West Coast, California, Inspector."

"Okay, and you had a few drinks?"

"Yes."

"And afterwards?"

"He was a bit drunk, me too. Well, we..."

"You did what, Mr Armstrong?" *It was DI Ling.*

"We had sex."

Sex. Yes, sex. Lovely sex.

"At your place, Mr Armstong?"

"I'm staying in a hotel, Inspector."

"At his?" *It was DI Ling.*

"If I may. We went to a park. Clapham Common."

"I see. Can you describe what he was wearing?"

"At the park?"

"Let's start with the bar, shall we?"

"Sorry, yes. Tight jeans, white T-shirt, denim jacket. Quite short blond hair."

"Okay, let me make a note." *It was DI Ling.*

Silence.

I remember you. It was a warm night. Lots of men in the pub. Lots in the park too. Others wanted to play. But you said no. You chose me, lovely American man, all for yourself. You chose me. I liked that.

"Okay, did he have anything with him? A wallet. A phone. A bag?"

"Who doesn't carry those things, Ma'am? I don't remember anything in particular."

"No bag? I mean, if you went to the … if you went for a walk together, you would have noticed a bag?" *It was DI Ling.*

"Yes, I guess. No bag."

"So, you had sex with this man?"

Yes, good sex. Hard sex. Punishing me.

"I believe it was him, officer. Can I plead the fifth amendment here?"

"We don't have that here, but you've not been charged with anything. Mitigating circumstances, as far as I'm concerned. Did you have sex with this man, at Clapham Common?"

"Yes. I had my own condoms."

"Mr Armstong, it is not my interest in what you do. I am merely trying to piece together Adam's movements the night before the attack. And the next day?"

"Thank you. I didn't go to the Pride Festival with him."

"So you know he went?"

"He said he was going."

"And when you had finished in the park, did you go back to the bar?"

"No. We parted there. Walked in different directions."

"And you didn't give him your name?"

"No."

"And did he tell you, perhaps, where he was going then? Where he was going to that evening? Where he was from? Where he would sleep?" *It was DI Ling.*

"No, we didn't speak too much at the park. He did say he was going to the Pride Festival, when we were in the pub. It was just what everyone was talking about."

"Unfortunately, Adam's clothes did not survive the blast. Is there any proof you can provide, that it was definitely this man that you met at the Two Brewers pub and had sexual relations with at Clapham Common?" *It was DCI Pierce.*

"He was wearing a cap on the night."

"Okay, a cap. Colour?"

"Er, blue maybe? Maybe, light blue?"

To hide my face. From God. From shame. From Dad.

"Okay, blue. Is that all?"

Yes, officer."

"Okay, well we'll take your details and we'll have to follow up. When do you go back to the States?" *It was DCI Pierce.*

"In a few days."

"And you'll be contactable though?" *It was DI Ling.*

"Of course. Anything I can do to help. Poor man."

"Thank you for your time, Mr Armstrong. And if you think of anything else?"

"Thank you, officer."

Door.

Silence.

Knock.

"Hello, officer?"

"Yes, Mr Armstrong." *It was DCI Pierce.*

"It's a bit embarrassing."

"Go ahead."

"Well, Adam - he has this little pattern of moles. A diamond of four, you know, on his back. Sorry, just, you did ask."

"That's very useful Mr Armstrong, thank you."

"Thanks."

Door.

"Well, what do you think?" *It was DI Ling.*

"Should we go back to the pub? Try to track down others who were at the Two Brewers that night?"

"And the railway stations?"

"Good idea. Let's get CCTV from Clapham Junction, Clapham North and Clapham?"

"Any sign of a man in a blue cap should do the trick, pinning David's movements before and after his meeting with Mr Armstrong."

"Good work, DI Ling. I'll ask a doctor or nurse in, to get an eye on those moles again."

"You'll probably need that responsible adult in too. Making sure you're not infringing the man's right to privacy."

"For goodness' sake."

27

Well, thank you Felicity and it does look like we have a very wet weekend ahead.

Yes, we're all going to need our wellington boots.

You're watching the Sunshine Sofa show, with me, Isha Khara.

And me, Edward Keaton.

We return now to the ongoing story of Adam Pound, or David as he's been known, who is in a coma at St Michael's hospital in London, following an explosion at the Pride Festival in June. This has been a complex story from the start, and it's just become more confusing.

That's right, Ed. The police are not saying why, but Adam's father was arrested yesterday for what they are calling 'suspected historical crimes'. Any ideas what that means, Isha?'

No idea, Ed, I guess we'll find out. But this comes at the same time as some court wrangling about Adam's right to die in hospital. The hospital has petitioned for Adam to be allowed to die if he has not recovered by June next year, by removing nutrition. However, Adam's parents have filed against this move in the courts, claiming it would be against their religion to allow Adam to die. Ed, what are the government saying?

Well, Isha, we asked the Home Office for an interview this morning on the case, but the Minister wasn't available. Instead, they provided a short statement:

'Our government expresses deep sympathy for all parties involved, however we rightly remove ourselves from decisions rightly made by doctors. It is for the hospital and the family to make representations.'

Today, we have Sir Bernard Loam on the Sunshine Sofa. He's a retired barrister with a history of arguing medical cases. Sir Bernard, can you explain, what happens when parents and hospitals disagree?

Well, this is a very unique case, because it really is rare for disagreement. Normally, in fact, the case would not even reach court. Legislation passed in 2018, in response to the case of Anthony Bland following the Hillsborough disaster, set the precedent that doctors could remove artificial feeding of a patient if the family consented.

But in this case, the family disagrees?

Yes, that is my understanding. Normally, the case would be heard in court, with each side represented. However, in this case social services has applied for a permanent restraining order against Adam's family.

Oh, that is new to us. Can you explain, Sir Bernard?

Well, I don't know the details, but the courts have put a temporary stop on parental responsibility for Adam, as a vulnerable adult, unable to make decisions for himself. So, decisions about his care fall to social services during that time. But the London Borough of Westminster have asked for a non-time limited extension of their responsibility for Adam.

So, in clear English, Sir Bernard, if I may: Adam's parents may lose the right to even argue that Adam should be kept alive?

I think it would be more complex than that, but theoretically yes. The Home Office statement before suggests the government doesn't have an opinion, but eventually they may have to intervene.

Thank you Sir Bernard. Now, Isha, I understand we've something delicious coming up on the programme later...

Door.

Dillon, is that you?

"Morning Adam, how's it going?"

What's wrong. You're quiet. You don't seem yourself.

"I won't stay long today, just calling in."

Oh, do you have a cold. Aren't you well?

Door.

Sleep.

Door.

"Good morning, oh, Mr Kendrick. Oh, goodness, what happened?" *It was Nurse Gail.*

"Shh, I was hoping to pop in here and get away quickly."

"What happened?"

"Some thugs. I got mugged. Well, beaten up, they didn't take anything."

"Thugs?"

"Not far from the hospital actually. It's nothing."

"Doesn't look like nothing Mr Kendrick. Should I take a quick look?"

"It's okay, I've spent the night in A&E downstairs. Thought I'd come up here early, see Adam, then go home and lick my wounds with..."

A&E, oh my Dillon, what happened?

"And you're straight up here? You should be resting surely?"

"I came to see Adam for his routine visit. Then I'll go home and sleep it all off."

"Here, let me look."

"That's kind of you. Oooh, that's..."

"Painful, I know. So, oh wow, that's one hell of a black eye."

"Really, it doesn't look that bad, does it?"

Oh, poor Dillon.

"I bet the other guy came off worse."

Silence.

"Oh, sorry. Inappropriate of me."

"No, its okay. Still trying to remember what happened. There were three of them. I may have managed the one."

"Mr Kendrick, that's awful. Where was it?"

"Down a back lane, on the way out of the hospital. I'm just glad it happened before I got home. Could have been much worse, if they'd have got inside."

"Did they take anything?"

"That was the thing. Or maybe not. Maybe they were just drunk. Didn't ask for my wallet or phone or anything. Just three guys... ow... thanks Gail... they just started laying about me with fists. I think they'd followed me from the hospital, waited until I walked down that dark part over the road?"

"So not mugged? Here, hold this plaster while I finish rewrapping your eye."

"Well, it was super weird actually. They kept calling me a queer. Faggot. That kind of thing. I should have fought back."

No, Dillon, never fight back. It only gets worse if you fight them.

"Oh, Mr Kendrick..."

"Please, you can call me Dillon."

"Dillon, that sounds like a hate crime. Will you tell the police that? How would they have known?"

"Known what?"

"Sorry, I mean, obviously they were just thugs. What the hell have we come to? Can't even walk down the street. There, all fixed up."

"Thanks Gail."

"And you will report it to the police?"

"Well, if DCI Pierce comes, I guess I'll have no choice. It's written all over my face."

"I mean, as a hate crime. We can't let them get away with it. The police take it more seriously if..."

"Okay, message received and understood. I'll tell them what I know. Three blokes. Fists. Blue Team. Then a kick in the face. Homophobic slurs. The full lot."

"Blue team, what's that?"

"Just what they shouted. No idea. Maybe their bloody football team, I'm not into the game."

"Well, maybe the police will know."

"Yeah, right you are. Ow, can you help me up, Nurse? I need to get home, my ribs are killing me."

"Did they give you medication downstairs?"

"A handful. I'm going to take them with half a bottle of Scotch."

"Not wise, Mr Kendrick..."

"Thanks Gail. Listen, I'll leave you to it. See you later. Bye Adam."

Door.

Blue team?

28

Door.

"Usual drill ladies and gentlemen. DI Ling, can you take notes?" *It was DCI Pierce.*

"Yes, Ma'am."

"All those present, state your names."

"Doctor Ann Atwan."

"Gail O'Connor, Nurse."

"DI Ling, Metropolitan Police."

"Dillon Kendrick, responsible adult, representing Adam Pound, patient."

"Thank you, Mr Kendrick. What happened to you?"

"I'll tell you later. Doesn't matter."

"That's your call. Well, I don't have much time. But I'm here to let you know before this becomes a media storm. I've already talked to hospital management about it."

"Hospital management?" *It was Doctor Atwan.*

"Yes, I'm afraid this involves the hospital."

"St Michael's?"

"Yes and security here. I'm afraid there's been another breach of Adam's security. You understand Mr Kendrick,

Doctor, that we've had CCTV in this room since Geoff Pound came in drunk and disorderly? For Adam's protection."

"I was not aware of that. I should have been told. Not only because I'm Adam's guardian, but also for my own privacy." *It was Dillon.*

"I'm sorry, Mr Kendrick, it was in police interest to set up the camera. Up there."

"Oh, God I can see it now."

"Sorry, Dillon, we should have been clearer. It's hospital policy to assist the police when there's a live investigation." *It was the doctor.*

"Well, I can't say I'm happy. I'll have to review it with social services."

Don't worry about it Dillon. I've nothing to hide here. Not from the police. Not from you.

"Fair enough, but I think you'll find what I have to show you enlightening. I brought some things to show you, Mr Kendrick and Doctor Atwan. I think to be fair, we needed to do this in the presence of Adam, as he's under your guardianship. It does directly pertain to his situation."

"Go ahead."

"Okay, well, here we have Adam's room, three days ago."

"What am I looking at, DCI Pierce? Can you turn the sound up." *It was the doctor.*

"There's no sound, and the picture isn't as clear as I'd like."

"What's this?" *It was Dillon.*

"Well, clearly three figures. They come in... here. Seem delighted with themselves. There's this one chap, pretty sure they're all male. He's standing at the door. I guess as a look out?"

"Okay."

"Now, watch. The other two go up to Adam's bed. They're really edgy, keep looking towards the door. Look, they're gesturing at each other. One of the guys, he's right up by Adam's head. Seems to be talking to him?"

Silence.

"Oh, my God." *It was Dillon.*

"Do you want me to stop the video?"

"No, no, it can wait."

"Here, and now the two are definitely arguing. Then, watch, the guy at the door. He gestures to the other two to leave. That's it, and they go."

"So, three strange men on my corridors..." *It was Doctor Atwan.*

"Wait, watch. Did you see that?"

"What? What did I miss."

"Let me scroll back. Here... just before they leave?"

"What? Are they punching the air? Celebrating?" *It was Nurse Gail.*

"No, look. Each of them, same hand, same gesture. It's more like a solid fist to their shoulder. Some kind of salute."

"Wow." *It was Dillon.*

"Wow, indeed."

"Why didn't I see this footage?" *It was Doctor Atwan.*

"We got permission from management. It's not a medical issue." *It was DI Ling.*

"Screw you officer, with all due respect." *Doctor, I like you more and more every day.*

"We have what we have." *It was DCI Pierce.*

"Who were these men?"*It was Doctor Atwan.*

"Here."

Shuffle.

"We had forensics blow up these images. I think you can all see on the left shoulder of each of these men? It's a badge. On this picture, from the guy right up against Adam's face, we can make out the letters 'Blue Team'."

Blue Team.

"DI Ling?"

"We arrested the three men at the Rose and Crown pub near Vauxhall last night. Suspicion of conspiracy to cause harm under the guise of gang violence. They call themselves *Blue Team*. It is our understanding that together they form a loose cell from a wider organisation of a particularly right wing persuasion. Not known for big extremist events, but there's always a first time."

"Wow, and they got into the hospital as a gang?" *It was the doctor.*

"It's certainly looking that way."

"My God, the media will go crazy. This hospital is full to the brim, they could have put everyone in danger."

"But they didn't, and I'm here to forewarn you about it. Your managers are already drawing up a strategy."

"Yeah, great. I don't believe I've ever met a hospital manager. They don't, you know, come down to the wards very often. How the hell did this happen?"

"We're going to have to leave that for another day. What's more important, is to identify how far they are a real threat: to Adam and the wider gay community." *It was DCI Pierce.*

"Mr Kendrick, are you okay?" *It was DI Ling.*

"It's real. They're for real. Can you get me some water, Gail?"

"Here."

"Go on." *It was DI Ling.*

"Those guys. Blue Team. It was them, the guys that mugged me. I'm sure of it. Homophobic slurs, the whole thing."

"I wondered where the bruises came from. Would you be prepared to make a statement?"

"Of course, DI Ling."

"You can come to the station later. Meantime, we are applying for an extension order to keep the men in for longer than the statutory two days, under terrorism legislation. We're looking into any connections they may have had with the bombing. It would be a long shot, but given they were here? But now, if true, we have an attack on Mr Kendrick on the basis of his sexuality. Given the homophobic attack, that might only strengthen our suspicions."

"Well..." *It was Dillon.*

"Terrorism?" *It was Doctor Atwan.*

"Yes, for the bombing."

"And they were in here? In this hospital?"

"Nurse Gail, could you ask if these men signed in to the ward? Perhaps they just sneaked in, but usually they'd have to come via the reception desk, isn't that right?"

"Usually."

"Okay, we're looking for a Mr Carl Pilkington, a Roger Parsons and..., okay, a Jason Lamb."

"Will do."

Whoah! Slow down. Not these guys, DCI Pierce. Ha ha, no, not these guys. They're not capable. I've known them since we were kids. Honestly, Jase Lamb! He can barely open a can of cider by himself. None of them would know hydrogen peroxide if it splashed them in the face. They couldn't smuggle a pair of underpants onto a tube train, let alone a bomb. I doubt they were the ones who hurt Dillon. Must have been someone else.

"I can't believe it." *It was Dillon.*

"Do I need to play it again?"

"Won't you need more evidence than that?" *It was Doctor Atwan.*

"Of course, that's why we're questioning them, and going right back to the beginning with what we now know. Now we have a clear ID on these *Blue Team* guys, we might just find their ugly faces in the crowd at Pride."

I guarantee you won't. You'll see. Dumb, Dumber and Dumber Still. Don't know up from down. God, they couldn't even figure out between their three brain cells that I was gay. And they've had years to work it out. It was just talk. I tolerated them, because Dad wanted me to have big masculine friends. They were a convenient hiding place for me.

"I'm completely shocked." *It was Dillon.*

"Who knows how these groups work. Encouragement. Support. Secrets. Winding each other up. The internet. But we're not shaping it in that way with the media, anyway. It's strictly about conspiracy, and possible membership of a prescribed organisation. We'll let the press do the speculating." *It was DCI Pierce.*

Murmuring.

"Good then."

Welcome to the afternoon show, this is Express News and I'm Sophie Horgan. Today, police say they have made significant progress in their enquiries into the London Pride bombing of 21st June. Our correspondent Dean Joyce reports from Vauxhall, South London.

Thank you Sophie. And yes, I'm standing outside the Rose and Crown pub, here on the banks of the Thames River. It was here, just a few hours ago, that officers arrested three men, who were known to be locals.

Six armed police officers were at the arrest, and no resistance was made. The police did not make a statement at the scene, though it is understood the arrests are connected to investigations into the 21st June bombing.

And Dean, do we have any idea who those men are?

Sophie, according to the locals I have spoken to here, the men met together in the pub regularly. One witness said the three men were a very tight group who jokingly called themselves Blue Team, perhaps a reference to Chelsea Football Club.

Pub goers said they were often rowdy, and had been asked to leave the pub on occasions because of inappropriate language, as well as for unruly behaviour. At this time, we are unable to name the men or confirm these claims.

Sophie, I spoke to the pub landlord, who said he has been asked to provide CCTV footage and a statement.

Thank you Dean Joyce. We turn now to Natasha Harding, our political editor, who has interviewed Peter Brookes, the father of Noor Hisham, the young woman who was previously suspected of setting off the device that killed 11 people and injured dozens more at the Pride Festival.

Yes, Sophie, my full interview will be broadcast as a special extension to this programme, this evening after the 6pm news.

But in my exclusive interview, Mr Brookes calls for the resignation of Home Office Minister Francis Gardiner.

Mr Brookes said the minister has failed to explain why his daughter was blamed for the bombing, and that his family have yet to receive an apology.

Mr Brookes also said the minister had pressured the police into finding a quick and easy suspect, which had led to his daughter being accused.

'For months, my gentle clever daughter was blamed by the Home Office, by the Metropolitan police, by the media and by the gay community and Black Lives Matter movement. We have not been able to grieve, and our hopes that the minister

would explain what went wrong in blaming my daughter have been crushed.

'So, I ask you, Mr Gardiner. What if it was your daughter and your family blamed for this horrific event? If you have the slightest regret over what you have said about my family, then you should resign immediately.'

Sophie, my programme has asked the government and Metropolitan Police for a response. The Metropolitan Police said it would not comment, due to the internal inquiry called by the Home Office.

The Home Office said no-one was available to respond this lunch time. I hope to hear from them by the time of broadcast this evening.

Back to you, in the studio.

29

Door.

"Judge Millar, please come through. It's good to see you again." *It was Doctor Atwan.*

"Thank you. Mr Kendrick. Nurse."

"And this is Ikana Okereke from Wandsworth social services."

"Hello. I'll just take a seat, if I may?" *It was the judge.*

"Judge Millar, thank you for coming to discuss Adam's case. As you know it's now been six months since Adam Pound first came into our care. We would like to continue our petition that he now be allowed to die humanely." *It was Doctor Atwan.*

"Well, I've already started work on my proposal. Have you completed the correct paperwork?"

"Yes, Judge."

"And Mr Pound's current health position?"

"He remains in a permanent vegetative state, Sir. The same as when he first came to us. We have never had any sign that he can hear us, or has any sense at all of even his own existence." *It was Doctor Atwan.*

"I see. And Mr Kendrick, you are still his representation here I see?"

"Yes, Judge. Though, of course, if this case proceeds, I understand it will be lawyers on behalf of Westminster and Wandsworth social services that will act. That is why Ms Okereke is here."

"Of course. Ms Okereke, am I to understand there are no next of kin?"

"No. The court of protection have put a stay on Mr and Mrs Pound's responsibility for him, as a vulnerable adult, due to suspicion of former child abuse. Mrs Pound was ruled to be under coersive control of her husband, so is not able to take responsibility."

"Convictions?" *It was the judge.*

"Sir, I believe the court of protection have jurisdiction without proven convictions." *It was Ms Okereke.*

"Arrests?"

"Sir, Mr Pound was arrested on suspicion of historical child abuse. He is currently on bail. Though the evidence against them is really quite strong. Strong enough for responsibility for Adam to be permanently removed." *It was Ms Okereke*

"I'm not so sure. I shall have to consult with the courts. This will add delay."

"Understood." *It was Doctor Atwan.*

"Any advanced decision? Any other power of attorney?"

Silence.

"I see the patient is no longer being fed through an oral tube, Doctor?"

"Sir, I installed a gastrostomy after his mother expressed concern." *It was Doctor Atwan.*

"Did you indeed? This mother who is now banned from seeing him? Very convenient."

"Would you like to see? I can pull back the covers."

"No, thank you very much. I have spent years as a medical solicitor. I've seen the results of enough medical procedures in my career."

"Me also." *Touché, Doctor Atwan.*

"Quite. Any other matters at hand?"

"Judge, there is a LGBTQ plus protest taking place next month in remembrance of the June bombing, and in support of Adam's right to die. I don't know if that makes any difference to your timescale?" *It was Ms Okereke.*

"I have no interest in this matter. I am concerned whether Adam Pound should have his nutrition removed."

"Sorry, I just thought. Well, if you've ever been to Pride, there are opposition protests too. Anti-LGBTQ plus. At this protest next month, there are likely to be anti-gay, right wing and right-to-life opposition protests. I think the tensions will be high between the groups."

"I have not been to Pride. Police will take care of the protests, surely?" *It was the judge.*

"More than ever. After all, they still haven't found the bomber." *It was Ms Okereke.*

Silence.

"We just wouldn't want any legal judgements about this case questioned. It could lead to accusations of undue influence from one or other side of the issue."

"I see where you're going. I can assure you I will be impartial and uninfluenced in my decisions. Once I have received all the evidence I want to consider."

"Just saying. The hospital's reputation and staff could be at risk."

Go for it, Ms Okereke.

"Very well. I shall see what I can do to bring forward my decision time. Hurry things along, as it were. But I do need clarity from the Courts of Ward on the status of Adam's parents. It is a shame you don't trust members of the judicial system to be impervious to outside influence."

"Thank you, Judge." *It was Doctor Atwan.*

"Meeting concluded I think. I'll let myself out."

"Thank you."

Door.

Silence.

Laughing.

"You didn't have to go in so hard on him, Ms Okereke. There are subtler ways of going about things." *It was Dr Atwan.*

"I thought it was what he needed?"

"You didn't need to push him. You just embarrassed him."

"I don't understand." *It was Dillon.*

"The talk of the feeding tube, did you miss it? He was checking that Adam was still being artificially fed. He reminded me, with just a look last time he came, that a patient who is orally fed cannot have feeding withdrawn. But if the tube goes into his stomach, it is entirely for medics to decide."

"Shit, he was already on board." *It was Ms Okereke.*

"Right from the start. We actually don't even *need* his legal opinion. Though I dare say management upstairs would be pretty terrified if we don't get that legal letter."

"So, it's going to happen. Adam will be allowed to die?" *It was Dillon.*

"One way or another."

"Finally. I can't believe it."

"Mr Kendrick?" *It was Doctor Atwan.*

"Well, finally - we're getting to the end of this. Poor Adam. He'll finally be set free."

Oh, Dillon, I do love you.

"Ah, Mr Kendrick, I hoped I'd find you here." *It was Nurse Gail.*

Sweet Nurse Gail.

"We've been getting a call to the nurses desk, asking to speak to the person responsible for Adam. We're usually able to weed out the cranks, but this guy seemed genuine. And he keeps calling."

"Okay."

"To be honest, I think he's been here, in the hospital before? Said his name was Carey Armstrong."

Carey Armstrong? I remember him. Sexy Carey. The Two Brewers in Clapham. Amercian.

"I'm not sure I remember him."

"Well, he wants you to call him back. He's left a number. I think he's in the States. I'll just get the number, shall I?"

"Can't do any harm can it, thanks Gail."

Door.

"Mystery man, Adam? I'm hoping it's not another of those journalists. Did you hear? The Blue Team guys? They were at football, of course. Couldn't have been the bombers. Video footage of them at the stadium, during the Pride Festival. They were drinking all day at the Rose and Crown before the match."

I did say. Dumb, Dumber and Dumber Still.

"Nasty lot though. Couldn't plant my mugging on them either. Their word against mine. I left it at that. Police gave them a caution for trespass on hospital property, the only thing they could do. Like water off a duck's back to them, no doubt."

I'm sorry Dillon.

"Well, I brought the paper."

What about the American? Are you interested in him, Dillon?

Door.

"Here you go. Best use your phone, rather than the hospital? Foreign number, etcetera."

"Of course, Gail."

Door.

"What do you think, Adam? Do you think he's after a date with you? Seems you made an impression on him last time?"

I remember him Dillon. Warm skin. In the trees, out there on Clapham Common. Sex. Forbidden sex. What would Dad think?

"The number is ringing. Foreign tone."

Good sex, Dillon. Though I felt guilty afterwards. Dad's voice going round my head.

"Oh, hi. My name is Dillon Kendrick. I'm calling from St Michael's Hospital in London. Yes, that's right, I'm responsible for David. Well, Adam Pound as it turns out. Yes, pleased to speak to you."

What's he saying, Dillon?

"I understand, no I can pass the message on. She's usually super busy, no wonder you can't get through. Urgent, okay?"

Silence.

Dillon?

"Er, okay. Give me that again, let me write it down. Green? Okay. Yeah, I've no idea. I guess we'll have to see. Okay, thanks for the details."

Ask him, Dillon.

"And she can reach you on the same number?"

Oh, get his details.

"No problem. Thanks Mr Armstrong."

Silence.

Dillon?

Silence.

Dillon, what did he say? What did the sexy man say?

"Well, that was weird. Better check with Gail when DCI Pierce is in next."

Dillon, what did he say?

30

Door.

"Adam, there's a big statement about you on the TV. They've been trailing it all day. Lots of speculation." *It was Marjorie.*

"Yes, come in Sheila, we can get it on the TV while we change his bed clothes."

Click.

"Oh, just the news for now."

We're expecting a statement from Metropolitan Police any time now, regarding Adam Pound, the last surviving victim of the Piccadilly Bomb, of the...

"Something about allowing him to die, I think maybe the authorities have made up their mind."

"Maybe that's why there's so many police around the hospital today. Whichever way it goes, someone's not going to be happy."

"Big day."

"Big day."

"Let's do his bed together, so we don't miss anything - and lift, that's it Adam - and just pull the sheets down, and release..."

"So what do you reckon, Marjorie?"

"What, if it was me?"

"Making the decision, not you lying here?"

"I think, poor Adam. He's been through enough. I think it's time to allow him to pass away."

"Tend to agree, Marj. But if it was your son?"

"Ah, thank God in Heaven it's not my son. Can't even go there. I'd like to say I'd let him go, but, well, its unthinkable."

"Oh, those poor parents."

"Aren't they supposed to be devout Christians, or whatever?"

"Doesn't make a difference, does it. They're still losing a son."

"Against their will, if the judges allow him to die."

"Or they might win, keep him alive. I heard they're still hoping for a miracle. That he's going to get better."

"Shame. Look at him, Sheila. Sweet boy. He looks so peaceful and settled, doesn't he? All his wounds healed up. He's not a bad looker, either. Now that all the bandages are off. He could be sleeping, if we didn't know better."

"So innocent."

"Shall I do the toilet?"

"No, look, here's that police woman now."

"Oh, get the sound up."

Thank you ladies and gentlemen for making the time this morning. I am Detective Chief Inspector Philippa Pierce from the Metropolitan Police, and as you will know I've been leading the investigation into the London Piccadilly Bombing on 21st June 2021.

I am joined here today by Bridget Soper, chief executive of Wandsworth social services. The reason for her presence here will soon become apparent, as I outline our findings here today. These are sensitive matters, and I hope members of the press will understand we are only able to say so much, and that questions must be kept to the minimum.

"Oh, Sheila, social services. Told you - they've made a decision. Looks like the parents have lost. Poor things. Poor Adam."

Is that it? Am I going to be let go? I want Dillon. Where is Dillon?

'If I may draw your attention, ladies and gentlemen, to the large screen to my right?

Snap, snap.

Yes, can we leave the photography for now? We shall be releasing what you see to everyone present.

What you are looking at is the green rucksack, from the Bigfoot store. We strongly believe a bag just like this was carrying the bomb when it went off, close to the Eros statue, during the Pride parade. If we can have the next slide please?

This image shows shards of fabric attached to nails and bolts, which have been identified as coming from that particular rucksack. And this large piece of fabric, also from a Bigfoot rucksack of the same type, was also found close to the scene of the bomb.

It was just behind where large fragments of the Black Lives Matter banner were found. That clearly indicates that the blast from the rucksack and the fragments of the banner were blown together, and in the same direction. This fragment of rucksack was found to have such intense doses of burned dioxins on it that it was likely to be either carrying, or at least extremely close to the device when it went off.

"This is exciting isn't it Marj? It's like watching Sherlock, or whatever?"

"Shouldn't we be getting on?"

"Just a few more minutes. I reckon everyone else in the hospital is watching just now."

As you are aware, we were able to eliminate a previous suspect from our enquiries, a young woman who was unfortunately killed in the blast. Once again, the Metropolitan Police would like to apologise for any confusion. We are in discussions with the Home Office about how information was released, but we express our deepest sympathy with those involved.

"She's milking it, isn't she Marj? It's like she's trying to delay saying something."

The retailer Bigfoot, as members of the press will be aware, provided a sample rucksack of the same type we suspected was carrying the bomb. You will have all received photos of that rucksack, and I would like to thank you all for distributing that image, and contributing to our enquiries.

"Get on with it."

"Shh. Poor Adam, why is she dragging it out? Let's get to the social services woman."

Ladies and gentlemen, what we were not informed of by Bigfoot at first, nor had we previously suspected, was that for a certain period just before Christmas, the same rucksack was sold with a promotional matching green cap. It was a so called 'Black Friday' offer, that was very successful and the retailer quickly ran out of caps.

This new information led to us making a more detailed search of photographs, CCTV and footage sent in by generous and helpful mobile device users at the Pride event.

If you turn your attention to the screen please? After many days of work by my colleagues, we have been able to identify that branded Bigfoot cap at the Pride Festival. Here, at the start of the march, at Green Park. And here, at the Mall, outside the Mercedes Dealership. Once once more, outside the Ritz Hotel.

Gasping.

As you will see, though the photograph is blurred, this rendition of a figure wearing the cap in question is standing an estimated twenty five metres in front of the Black Lives Matter banner. Though we cannot be sure of it, on closer examination, the figure appears to have two patches at the shoulder that match the colour of the cap. As I said, we cannot be sure, but we strongly suggest these are the two arm straps of the rucksack in question.

Snap. Snap. Snap.

Please, as I said, you will get these images.

Sally Rider, The Mercury, do you know who's wearing the cap, Detective Chief Inspector?

I have asked for patience from the press, Ms Rider. If you don't mind. I'm on national TV as I understand it. You're not going to get your scoop before anyone else.

Snap. Snap. Snap

"She's obviously distressed. Look at her, Sheila. All red in the face. Poor love."

"What's she hiding, Marj?"

"Wow, this is exciting. Adam, I wish you could see this."

We have analysed footage and photographs of the march, as it progressed towards Piccadilly Circus. At this point, just ten metres from the statue of Eros there, we see the figure again. Notice, there are no straps on the shoulders. We have two images to compare?

Snap. Snap. Snap

And if we take another still from CCTV, from outside the former Trocadero centre, this figure here - now known to be Noor Hisham - she has picked up the rucksack. I shall not play it, but on audio recording from mobile phone footage at this time, a woman's voice can be heard asking if anyone knew, and I quote, 'who this bag belongs to?' It was moments after this that the explosion went off.

Click, click, click. Gasp.

Okay, a moment of calm please, ladies and gentlemen. Thank you. You'll receive a full statement.

"Oh, my god. She's going to reveal who the bomber is. You're going to get justice Adam."

Re-examination of the footage, and discussions with Bigfoot, lead us to strongly suggest that the wearer of the cap was very likely to be the one carrying the rucksack that carried the bomb. From there, we were able to do a number of things.

First, we were able to trace the figure wearing the cap to London Underground stations. Here getting off the tube at Lancaster Gate. Earlier, getting on the Underground network at Vauxhall. And here, changing tubes at Oxford Circus.

And if we close in on those photographs.

Ahh, wow...

"Oh, my God Sheila."

And secondly, we have identified the same figure with the same cap at a bar in Clapham the night before, both from the bar's footage here. And from Clapham South tube station, here. We also have witnesses from the bar, including a witness who contacted us directly, who had close contact with our suspect, during that evening.

Click, click, click.

"No, it can't be."

"I feel sick."

Ladies and gentlemen, I must ask you to take a seat. Our investigations have concluded that our main suspect for the bombing of London Piccadilly Circus on 21st June 2021 is Adam Pound.

Door.

"Excuse me?"

"Oh, officer, sorry. We're just cleaners."

"Can I see your identification please? Okay, I'm going to have to ask you to leave this room immediately."

"Yes, no problem officer, we were just..."

"Now please, ladies."

And before I take any questions, I'd like to introduce Bridget Soper, chief executive of Wandsworth social services, who hopes to explain the legal situation with regards to...

Click.

Silence.

Door.

No. No, it can't be. Dillon, where are you? Please, help me.

Please, I didn't do it.
I'm innocent. I'm innocent.

"Adam, I don't understand this. I'm not supposed to be here right now. But I need to let you know, quickly. For some reason the police. They're thinking you set off the bomb. I don't get it. I don't at all. Surely not?"

No, Dillon. I didn't. How can they think that?

"DCI Pierce told me she needs to work out what my role is, if they want to pursue that line of inquiry. I'm not supposed to see you until then, Adam. I just can't believe that, and I suppose I should represent you whatever, but honestly Adam? A bombing?

"All those people? It can't be you? I mean, you've had sex with those men. That Carey Armstrong from the phone call. You were at the Pride Festival. I need to understand, Adam. I'm sorry, it's selfish of me, but please I need to believe you didn't do it."

I didn't do it, Dillon. I can't have done. I'm gay, Dillon. You know I can say that now. Now I'm free.

"Oh David, I mean Adam, how can it be? I think it's an easy win for them. To pin it on you Adam. Take the pressure off from the Home Office. The Foreign Office. Like they did with Noor Hisham. You know? Got the criminal. He's incapacitated. End of story. Justice served."

Hold me. Tell me it'll be okay. I didn't kill all those people. I love those people. I need them. I need you.

"Oh, Adam, I don't know what to do to help you."

Door.

"Shit."

"Mr Kendrick, what are you doing here?"

"Just saying goodbye, DCI Pierce."

"I told you to step back from Mr Pound here. Or did I not make myself clear?"

"Yes, sorry. I just thought."

Dillon, don't go. I need you still.

"Don't think. Just remove yourself from this room. Next time, I will have you arrested for interfering with police investigations."

"Has there been progress?" *It was Dillon.*

"Must I ask an officer to come in to remove you, Mr Kendrick?"

"No, sorry. I have to go Adam."

No, don't go.

Door.

Silence.

Knock.

Door.

"Oh, for goodness sake. What?"

"Inspector?"

"Ah, yes, sorry. Doctor Atwan. Thanks for coming in. And here's DI Ling. Have you met Ms Okereke from Wandsworth social services. She'll be standing in as representative on behalf of Adam Pound? His responsible adult."

"Pleased to meet you."

"Okay, DI Ling can you please begin recording."

"Ma'am."

"Doctor Atwan, Ms Okereke, we have reason to believe that Adam Pound, known previously by this hospital as David, may have been responsible for the explosion at the London Pride Festival on 21st June."

No, no it can't be true.

"Due to his current state, we are not able to charge him, but it is our intention to pursue this line of inquiry and announce to the public we are no longer looking for another suspect. Our investigations will then be closed.

"Closed, DCI Pierce?" *It was Doctor Atwan.*

"I'm presuming your recommendations are already to remove life support for Mr Pound, on the grounds of his impossibility of recovery? Is that process in motion?"

"That is likely to be the conclusion of the courts, yes. And yes, it is likely to be the conclusion of hospital managers."

"Then we all win, don't we?" *It was DCI Pierce.*

Oh, my goodness.

"There'll be a social media massacre? Don't you need to prove the case." *It was Okereke.*

"It'll die down, and there will be a conclusion."

"But what are the grounds for your suspicion?"

"CCTV at Clapham Junction on the morning of the bombing. Adam wearing a green cap, and carrying a green rucksack. Both with the Bigfoot brand on them. That's the rucksack we identified as carrying the explosive device. We have CCTV evidence of him approaching the parade late in the day, rather than at the beginning. And being so close to the bomb that his feet were blown 10 or 15 metres away from the Black Lives Matter banner. No one at the parade came forward, claiming to know Adam, indicating he was not really an active part of the gay community. Normally, people would go with friends, wouldn't they?"

"Surely that's conjecture. Is it enough to prosecute?" *It was the doctor.*

"Like DCI Pierce has said, we don't need to prosecute in this situation." *It was DI Ling.*

"But if Adam was sentient?"

"That might be a different matter. But we are where we are."

"Very neat for you, what with the Saudis putting on the pressure on the government for the bombing to be solved?" *It was Okereke.*

"All other avenues have run dry, I think this is a fair enough conclusion."

"So, that's that, then? I can inform managers to begin court proceedings to allow Adam to die?" *It was Doctor Atwan.*

"The public will be baying for his blood the moment I make the announcement that our investigations are over. Better he goes the humane way, and we get this closed down as soon as possible."

Silence.

"I'll wait a few days. But we all know where this is going. Meeting concluded, I think."

Wait. Is that it? I didn't do it! I didn't DO IT! How could I? It wasn't my rucksack. I found it, I'm sure I did.

Dillon, help me. It wasn't me.

31

Welcome back to the morning show, and the Sunshine Sofa. Though things don't feel quite so sunny today with the revelation of the new suspected identity of the Piccadilly Bomber, announced by the Metropolitan Police last night.

That's right, Isha. It's hard to believe, but in a shocking turn of events, the Detective Chief Inspector in charge of the case announced yesterday that all attentions were now turned to 'David', the man who was left unconscious, and unable to move, hear, speak or communicate after the bomb.

Isha, my understanding is that police believe Adam Pound, a 25 year old coffee shop and garage worker from Tooting Bec, South London, may have planned and executed the attack as a hate crime against homosexual people, and also against people of colour Isha.

Yes, that's right Ed. It was hard to watch: The Inspector in charge of the case showed images a man in a cap, and carrying a rucksack, which they say carried the bomb. That rucksack was then dropped in the road during the Pride event, only to be picked up by Noor Hisham, who was originally, and completely innocently, blamed for the bombing.

Oh, it's such a mess, isn't it?

Well, this morning we have Noor Hisham's dad with us, Peter Brookes on the Sunshine Sofa. Thanks, Mr Brookes for coming in. This must be very hard for you?

Thanks for having me on. Yes, it was difficult to watch yesterday. Though a relief in some way.

Peter, may Isha and I express our deepest sympathy. For weeks, your family was subject to abuse and investigation. Is that right?

We were. Police jumped to conclusions, and within a few days my innocent daughter was strung up for a crime she didn't commit. She was beautiful, intelligent and loved knowledge. That's the only reason she got interested in Islam. She was curious, but that was enough for the media and the police to try and convict her in the public eye.

Again, we're very sorry for your loss, Mr Brookes. It must have been horrific for you?

Of course. Charlotte left that morning happy. She was carrying a Pride placard she'd made herself. We gave her our Christian blessing, though we understood she was doing this in her new persona as a Muslim. We were proud of her. Sorry...

Please take a moment.

We tried to tell the police after the bomb. We were proud of our little girl. Standing up for the rights of minorities. And then we heard about the explosion. It's the worst thing anyone can go through, and then we found out. Oh, my God, we found out because she wasn't answering her phone, and she hadn't posted on Instagram after the bomb.

I'm sorry.

It was so hard. Because we only had two days to grieve. They wouldn't let us see her body. Said they were investigating. And then, out of the blue, no one even asked us, they started saying she did the bomb. Publicly announced it.

My sweet little girl? Can you understand that. The police came round, but not to protect us. They wanted to search our house. Charlotte's room, her laptop. We were victims of the bomb, but we were treated like we'd done it ourselves.

And the public. The media. Even our neighbours. Everyone had something to say. Or deliver through our mailbox. It was disgusting. And we'd just lost our daughter.

And how do you feel now, now that the police have announced they suspect Adam Pound carried out the bombing.

Angry. Really angry. How could they have missed a right wing plot? It was so obvious. Adam must have been a cruel and angry man. He deserves everything he has suffered. Dying in that bomb would have been too good for him. I'm glad he's suffering. I only hope he really can hear. And later, I hope he recovers, so he can see the damage he's done to everyone. To my family. To everyone's family.

Are you okay, Mr Brookes. Ed, should we cut to an advert?

Adam, I have no sympathy for you. Not an ounce. I wish you the worst. I wish you and your family everything we went through ten times over. Because you are a coward. My daughter stood up for her rights and those of her friends. You dropped a bomb, killed eleven people and tried to run away. Well, I'm glad you didn't escape.

Ed?

Okay, I think we will move to a break just now. Here's a few messages, and when we get back, we'll be hearing about our weather forecaster's latest adventures on Lake Windermere.

Mr Brookes...

Click.

"Oh Adam, what did you do?"

It was Nurse Gail. Are you crying Nurse?

"I've looked after you. I thought you were a sweet man.

How could you kill all those people. Your warped mind, your crazy beliefs?"

Gail, I don't understand. Please, hold me. Touch me.

"Well, listen to me you murderer, in the name of my children and my sister, I'm going to give you minimum of care from now on. I'll do my job, because I am true to my vocation, but that's it. No special treatment, no friendly chats. I'm going to stick to visiting times only for your boyfriend. If he ever comes back."

Gail, no. Not Dillon. He'll want to see me, won't he? Please, he's all I have.

"God, Adam. What have you done to all of us. You bastard."

Bash.

Are you punching me, Nurse?

Bash.

Bash.

"Oh, God. You bastard, Adam. You bastard."

Crack.

What was that?

Crack.

Again.

Patter, patter, patter, crack.

Door.

"Quickly, let's move his bed away from the window. Charlie, can you shift his monitors."

Who is that?

Click. Clunk.

"Okay, help me shift the bed. Close to this wall as possible."

Crack. Patter, patter.

"Has someone called the police?"

"The duty reg has. Security are on their way up."

Clank.

"Okay, fastened. What's the protocol on this?"

"Don't know. It's not a terrorist attack or a fire, or anything we've practiced for. I guess we'll wait for the police."

Crack.

"Eeek."

"Its okay, Maria. I think that's double glazing. Nothing is going to get through it from that height."

"You sure."

"I'll get some panels if I can find some. Put them up against the window."

"Good idea."

Silence.

"Charlie."

"Nurse."

"Does he deserve this? I mean, you know what the police said. He might be the bomber, and all that."

"I'm just an orderly."

"Yeah, but, I mean, you know. If it was your daughter. If they'd been hurt, you know, in the bomb?"

"I can't even think about it."

"But would you. Would you be on that protest downstairs? Would you be throwing rocks?"

"Man, if it was my kid?"

"Yeah, or your wife or whatever? It's okay, don't answer."

"I better go get those panels."

"Sure Charlie."

"You okay here. You know, with the stones? And with the patient."

"Yeah, of course, Charlie."

"Okay, back in a minute."

Door.

Footsteps.

"Adam, you fucking piece of shit. If I had my way, I'd open the window and throw down a rope ladder. Point to the fucking off switch."

Loud. Very loud. Right in my face loud. Who are you?

"The worse thing is, I cried for you. Me and the other nurses. We felt sorry for you. You had us all fooled, didn't you? Coward. Didn't even have the guts to kill yourself in that bomb. You tried to run away, didn't you, Shithead. You gave your rucksack to that poor girl. You had us all fooled."

Crack.

"But you'll find justice, you cretin. Because what you're going through right now? That's going to feel like a birthday party when they ship you to the Saudis."

The Saudis?

Patter, patter, patter. Crack.

Door.

"Oh, hello. Nurse, I'm PC Khalid Khargi, can I ask you to step away from the patient, and keep clear from that window please. We need to secure this room."

"Yes, of course, officer."

Sirens. Lots of sirens.

"I'm going to stand guard at the door, Nurse. Do you have any further business with your patient here?"

"No, officer, I think I'm finished with him. Completely finished."

"Okay, thank you. Could you make me a list of any people who should have access to the patient, on an official basis?"

"I'm just a night cover, officer. But I'll find out what I can."

Door.

Silence.

Crack.

Crack.

Chanting.

32

Door.

"Okay, here we are. Adam, I've someone to introduce you to. Let me just get the curtains there."

It was Nurse Gail. Where's Dillon?

"David, this is Rita. She's going to be your responsible adult for a while. Rita, this is David. Well, his real name is Adam, but we're so used to calling him David."

"What, you talk to him?"

Where's Dillon? Doesn't he want to see me?

"Well, we've tended to. It's something Dillon did, and it kind of just caught on for some of us. Of course, it's been tougher since, well, you know since we found out about him. It's totally up to you."

"I don't think I will."

"Fair enough. You know what you're doing?"

No, please, talk to me? Like Dillon did. Tell me where he is.

"Yes, Nurse. This is hardly the first medical case I've sat in on."

"Okay, fine."

"When do you expect the doctor to come on his rounds?"

"Doctor Atwan will be around the wards soon. But *she* will be looking at urgent cases first."

"No problem. I've brought a book to get me through a couple of hours, if it takes that long."

"Well, anything you need?"

"A cup of tea would be nice?"

"A cup of tea?"

"No milk or sugar, if you haven't got camomile?"

"Erm, well I'll have a look. After I've seen my own patients."

"No, that's fine. Of course, in your own time."

"Okay."

Door.

Where's Dillon? Talk to me, tell me where Dillon has gone? Why is he not coming to see me?

"Now, let's see, where was I... Ahah. The lights are so dull in these hospital rooms."

Good morning, welcome to those who've just joined us. Well, incredible revelations this week, Isha?

Yes, Ed. The police are now saying that Adam Pound was definitely responsible for the bombing of the Pride Festival on 21st June. The same Adam who was at the parade himself, and had been spotted in gay bars being intimate with other men, and now revealed as having had sexual relations with a gay man, the night before.

So, we're lucky enough to have our political editor Natasha Harding on the Sunshine Sofa. Good morning Natasha.

Good morning.

And Aaron Dixon from The Times.

Good morning.

Aaron, before we start, we have to ask you about your new puppy, what's her name?

Thatcher.

Oh yes, Thatcher. Here she is, a little picture taken from your Instagram, Aaron. She's a real cutie.

The newest member of our family.

What is she?

A Biewer Terrier. She basically does whatever I tell her to do.

Ha, a proper lapdog?

Yes, thank you Isha. But she's not quite got the house rules yet.

Well, her namesake never did quite get into line, did she?

Ha, ha. Well, she sure is a cute one. Now, Ed, on a more serious note.

Yes, Isha, the papers are full today of the news that police suspect the man previously known as David, who was heavily injured in the Pride bombing at Piccadilly Circus, actually set off the bomb himself. Natasha Harding, what are the papers saying?

Thank you, Ed. Well, according to the morning papers, and backed up by my own sources in the Home Office, the Metropolitan Police say Mr Pound acted alone. It was initially thought that the right wing activist group Blue Team supported his actions, but it has become clear that the men who were initially arrested could not have been responsible.

Mr Pound's own father, Geoff Pound, has also been excluded from the investigation. You will remember, Geoff Pound was held briefly by police on unrelated charges relating to suspected historical crimes. He was on a Christian retreat, at the time of the bombing.

So, Aaron Dixon, deputy editor at The Times?

Well, our headline says it all, doesn't it? 'Adam should face justice'. We're leading on the idea that Adam should be publicly prosecuted and tried for the bombing.

That's a contradiction to your previous call for Adam to be allowed to die. You said it was all politics.

Well, we've all been confused by this story, Isha. It's very fast moving.

But isn't that against the law: I think Adam can't be tried, because he doesn't have any consciousness.

The Home Secretary has the power to prosecute, despite his condition. I think the public need to see justice being done. This was a horrific crime.

Hold on.

Our political editor, Natasha Harding. Please go on?

Yes. Some would argue the man is suffering enough? He was caught up in his own bomb, if indeed he did set it off. He wouldn't be able to plead guilty if he did. Last week you were appealing to allow him to die.

We don't have the death penalty in the UK, Natasha.

So, let me get this right, Aaron.

Go ahead, Ed.

Last week you were saying let him die out of sympathy. And this week, you're saying force him to live as a punishment. And because we don't have the death penalty, that's the only way we can proceed? Is that right?

It seems simple to me. Adam needs to be held to justice in the public eye. If convicted, he should be held in a medical prison for his crimes, for the rest of his life. If found innocent, then it will be for the ward courts to determine his fate.

Well, thank you Natasha Harding. And Aaron Dixon, from The Times. This story looks like it's going to continue to run for the time being. And Aaron, do give Thatcher a little squeeze from all of us. Shall we have another little look at her? There she is.

So cute.

Can't wait to get back to her.

Well, we'll see you again, and we'll see you our audience after the break. And do send in your opinion on this debate via our social media channels.

Or cute pictures of your own doggy...

Stop it, Isha, we'll be inundated.

"Adam?"

Oh Dillon, you've come back to me.

"Oh, David. Adam. Whatever your name is. Shit, I don't even know."

Are you still my boyfriend?

"I've come to see you, but I'm not quite sure why. Ms Okereke wanted me back in, said it would give you consistency. DCI Pierce isn't delighted, but there's nothing she can do. She said it didn't matter, but you can tell she's pissed off."

I'm glad you're here.

"The thing is, I'm confused. I don't now what to believe."

Please, I'm confused too. I don't remember that day. The bomb has exploded my memories. I remember the night before. I remember the American. And I remember waking up, with you at my side. You've been strong for me.

"I don't understand it. You had sex with that guy, Armstrong. He confirmed it. You're gay, Adam. You hang around in gay bars. You sleep with men. Your dad obviously hates that you're gay."

I am gay, Dillon. I'm gay, and I want to be with you.

"I must be missing something. But I've come back. God

knows why, but I've come back. I have this inkling. I can't pin it down. I thought being with you, maybe a few more times, would help. An inkling about why you did it. What was going through your mind?"

Could I have done it, Dillon?

"Will you help me, Adam? If we sit still? If we just be here, together. Can you, I don't know, give me an idea? Something in me wants me to work it out."

I want to work it out too. We'll do it together.

"I think if I can understand, then maybe - maybe I'll know the way forward. You know, with the doctors and the courts. How to do my job properly?"

I promise, Dillon. I promise. I'll try harder to remember.

33

On the Sunshine Sofa this morning, we'll be talking about gay pride, and how some gay men and women don't actually support Pride and what it stands for.

That's right, Isha. This comes in the wake of the revelation that Adam Pound, a 24 year old man who was known to have sex with men, may actually have set off the bomb at the Pride Festival last June, killing 11 people and hurting many others. Adam, or David as he was known to medical staff, remains in an unrecoverable vegetative state at St Michael's Hospital in London.

We must emphasise that the police are unable to charge Mr Pound with the bombing, because of his medical condition, and have asked the public not to speculate about the man's motives for the bombing.

Now, I remember when I was younger and at university in East London, well we'd go along to the Pride Festival because it was fun, Isha. All the colours and the crowds. It really brought London to life. I'm not gay, as my wife I hope will attest to, but we went with friends, some of whom were gay, to enjoy the vibe. It was great to see so many on the tube wearing rainbow ribbons, and slogan T-shirts and carrying balloons. I mean, how often do any Londoners get to get together for a party like that?

Ah, well New Year's Eve, Ed. And the Notting Hill Carnival.

We used to go to that, too, Isha. Anything for a party.

Well, yes. But it seems, not everyone is delighted with the idea of Pride. Here to discuss the matter on the Sunshine Sofa is psychologist, Rowan Finch, himself a gay man, and an outspoken member of his community. Mr Finch, I understand you yourself are not keen on gay pride as a concept?

Thanks for having me on. That's right, I've never been particularly in favour of Pride, at least not since it became more of a celebration than a march for rights.

Can you tell us more?

Well, Pride separates LGBTQ plus people from the communities around us. It emphasises our differences, if you like. But haven't we, since the 60s or even before that, been demanding equality? Now we've achieved it, we want to be treated as if we're special.

Do you know how many police have to be taken off duty so we can parade around London? It's like we're more valuable than straight people. That's just too far to go the other way. And by the way, I may be gay Isha, and thanks for introducing me that way, but really - is that the most interesting thing about me?

Oh, no offence meant, I hope you understand that, Mr Finch.

The thing is, to be honest, I'm not sure I feel anything to be proud of these days. Men dressed up in drag? How's that not misogynist? Why do gay men have to imitate women? Wearing makeup, prancing around in sparkly dresses, bending their wrists, basically making themselves look feminine. If I was a woman, I'd take offence.

I believe many do, particularly with transexuals and transpeople?

Right, Ed. And when I was at school, if you were a boy, being called a girl was an insult. God forbid you were a bit camp. We do ourselves no favours by acting that way.

And do you know what else, I think it puts straight people off. We're like monkeys in a zoo, something to be gawped at. No offence, Ed, but you went to Pride to have a fun party around the gays. It's embarrassing.

These are very strong views, Mr Finch. Do you think they're widespread in the gay community.

That's another thing, Ed. The gay community? Like we're all one, slot in, be camp, scream a bit, go to filthy nightclubs. God, we're generating our own stereotypes. The behaviour of gays in night clubs? I don't know if you've ever been to one, but, well it's tantamount to sexual assault sometimes. Certainly not something you'd see or accept in a straight club. Only, we celebrate the endless groping. We laud those who go seeking 'chicken tonight'.

Chicken?

It's gay slang. It means a younger man. Like a virgin or something. I mean, why do we even have gay clubs if we're so equal? We're supposed to be past all that. What we are doing is creating and then celebrating stereotypes that the majority of people hate: camp, drag, butch bears, gay saunas, cottaging, transgender, an obsession with sex and bodies. It gives more ammo for people to do us down. There's a London club called 'Fist' for God's sake. Why can't we just calm it down and get on with our lives?

Mr Finch, do you believe Adam could have shared some of these views. Could that have been what motivated him?

Are you asking me because I'm a psychologist, or because of what I've just said?

Sorry, again, didn't mean to offend.

No, it's okay to offend. I wouldn't be here if things I said didn't offend. Your Twitter feed should be going mad. Oops, not allowed to say 'mad' either. Anyway, I don't know Adam's case. I am gay, but do I regret being gay? Yes, absolutely. I would love to have been straight. I'm not proud. I'm ashamed. Not because of who I am, but because of the behaviour of those who claim to represent me.

And I don't think I'm a minority. I think there are a lot of gay people out there who wish this whole obsession with being out and proud, would just go away.

And your professional opinion on Adam?

Well, I would never support violence, if that's what he actually did. I guess we'll never know. But I totally understand the anger and frustration. Some of us, especially when we were younger, wanted to keep being gay to ourselves. And then we were pushed into positions that forced us to come out. It was not acceptable to be ourselves.

My understanding was that Adam didn't want to express his sexuality. That he was committed to his church. Why couldn't he have been left alone, to do what he wanted to do? No, instead, we have to publicly be gay and that makes me cross. It makes me very cross indeed.

Thank you, Mr Finch. Well, we'd welcome your comments on this topic, at the usual...

Door.

"Adam, I think I have it. I think I finally understand."

Boyfriend?

"Listen, do you remember that Rachel Jones? The one whose column we like. I read her this morning. I think I get it. It all adds up. Your dad. The church. Blue Team."

Talk to me Dillon.

"She's usually pretty level, and certainly not scared of her own shadow. I'd like to believe what she's saying. I hope I'm not kidding myself. I want to look into it more. I mean, it could explain everything. If she's right, I might be able to move forward with you."

How can you stand to be with me? I still don't understand why I did it?

"So, where are we? Okay, here. It's in The Times. I looked online, and the comments underneath were pretty harsh. But still, listen: 'Being gay in today's society can lead to feelings of self-disgust and self-hatred. According to psychologists, this self oppression frequently leads to internalised homophobia.'

"Wow, that's quite a statement. Did you hear that? Internalised homophobia. I didn't know gay people could hate themselves?"

Oh, we can Dillon. And the people around us.

"'The result can be severe mental distress, including low self-esteem, contempt and loathing for the out LGBTQ plus community, and' - listen to this Adam - 'engaging in homophobic behaviour, including physical attacks. If Adam Pound felt that way, it is no surprise that a warped sense of his own worth could lead to the worst of outcomes.'

"Oh, my God, Adam. Is that what this was? Were you so ashamed of yourself, that you wanted to punish everything gay you encountered?"

Dad wanted me punished. It's all I believed in.

"And here, Adam, 'Psychologists link self-hatred due to

homosexuality closely with depression, alcoholism and substance abuse, shame and suicidal thoughts.'"

The drink. The drugs. The Rose and Crown. The shame after sex. I remember it, Dillon, I remember it.

"And here, 'Gay men will remain in abusive relationships, or in relationships they don't want, because to attempt to escape plunges them into the reality of their sexuality and the discrimination they will face. Instead, they hope a same sex relationship, or remaining closeted in their own community, will somehow cure them of their sexual feelings.'

"Listen to this. She's spot on I think: 'We should look at all events such as the Pride bombing in the same way. Look not only at the individuals directly involved, but those who influence them, the challenges they've faced, and the desperation they've felt in their own lives. No individual is completely and entirely to blame for their actions, whether good or bad. To call them simply evil is a weak get-out-clause for those of us who want a quick fix. Instead, we should look with sympathy and openness at where those actions came from.

"'We should examine everything from their social media account, to their upbringing, the religious beliefs they held and were forced to hold, and the treatment they have received for being who they are. In Adam's case, the influence of his strict religious upbringing should not be discounted. In fact, as more is revealed about the actions Adam's own parents carried out on him, they may perhaps be the most significant factor in the events of 21st June last year. The context of the cult-like religion to which his parents belong is not insignificant.

"'A bomber is never just a bomber for bombing's sake. And an extremist never an extremist for extremism's sake.

They come from somewhere. And that somewhere is more complex than we can ever imagine.'

"Adam, do you think she's right? Is that what happened to you?"

Oh Dillon, I think I understand. I'm gay. I must be because I love you. I have no right to be happy, but the only thing keeping me alive right now is that you love me.

How could you spend time with a monster like me. After what I've done. I didn't know, Dillon, I really didn't.

The memory does strange things. Strange things when your brain has been rocked in your skull, and half carved out of your head by shrapnel. Strange things when you bang your forehead so hard on the ground, you have to learn up from down, right from left all over again. In the dark. In the loneliness.

Strange things when all you hear is that you were the victim. The innocent. That you have had the worst of luck. That they will find the person who did this to you.

Strange things when you're loved by people who never loved you before. Supported by strangers. Adored by people who don't know you and before didn't care. People hold vigils outside of your window, calling you a hero.

Because suffering a little bit, over a long time isn't enough, Dillon, is it? The daily strappings. The burned feet. The empty meal times. The shunning of my dad's withering looks. The shunning of God. No one cares about that suffering.

The pain that being gay can be, when it's the worst pain in the world.

It took days to learn to build a bomb. It took years to learn to hate being gay. To hate so intensely that I wanted to destroy everything that I was, and everything that was around me. Being gay has destroyed my life.

And now they do hate me, don't they? Because I lay here in secrecy, didn't I? Pretending to be a victim. They felt hoodwinked. Kidded. Tricked. I didn't move a muscle. And I never even spoke.

And the worst thing is: now I know I can love you, and that you love me, I don't want to destroy. I want to love.

Oh, God, I wish we could start again.

34

"Do we have to do this here?"

I've heard that voice before.

"Yes, Minister Gardiner. Adam has a right to be involved in discussions about him. Dillon, if you will." *It was Doctor Atwan.*

"Oh, don't stand. I won't be long."

"Sorry, I'm Dillon Kendrick. I'm Adam's responsible adult."

"His guardian?"

"No, sorry, Sir..."

"In lieu of his parents as carers, we're appointed as social services to look after Adam's interests." *It was Ms Okereke. Oh, I'm glad you're here.*

"Really? The interests of a terrorist? Tax payers pay for that?"

"I believe that's government policy, Sir." *Good old Okereke.*

"Everyone has a right to a fair hearing, Minister. Dillon is a volunteer. He does a lot for society."

"Thanks, Doctor." *It was Dillon.*

"Where's the police? There should be police here."

"They're at the door Minister. This is a welfare matter, not one about prosecution."

"Madness. When I last came, he couldn't hear. Is that still the case?"

"Sir, we've been behaving as if Adam can hear us all. We think it's better to give him the benefit of the doubt." *It was lovely Dillon.*

"Okay, I guess I need to get into your headspace. In my mind the man is a terrorist."

"This is a hospital, Sir. We are concerned with the health and welfare of patients, whatever their status." *It was Doctor Atwan.*

"No, no. I understand that. I'm under a lot of pressure. I'll try to be a little more reasonable."

"Thank you." *It was the doctor.*

"So, I have a very busy schedule, including ten minutes with the PM this afternoon. Last time I was here I was apologising to this man's parents. What can I do for you?"

"Sir, we want your consideration, as Home Office Minister, to back our decision to allow Adam Pound to die. Here, in custody of the hospital. He is totally incapable, by our understanding is not aware in any degree, no memory, no thoughts, no feelings." *It was Doctor Atwan.*

"But he's a bomber."

"Possibly, not convicted." *It was Ms Okereke.*

"The police seem pretty sure."

"But they can't prosecute him, so effectively he remains innocent until proven guilty. It's a moot point, because he's effectively already brain dead."

"It may be a moot point to you, Ms Okereke, but I have responsibility to the public. Let me think for a moment.

What's the convention, if patients are not convicted of a crime?"

"Convention is that patients in his situation are allowed to pass away, under human rights legislation." *It was the doctor.*

"But I think this might be different, because of the special circumstances. The Home Office has powers here." *It was the minister.*

"Sir, please have some compassion." *It was Dillon.*

"I'm sorry?"

"Compassion."

"I'm very sorry, Mr Kendrick. You need to look at this in a wider context. Everyone on the other side of that wall thinks this is a man who has killed 11 people because of his hateful views. Injured hundreds. Caused community tensions. My government blames him for tensions between us and good friends of this country."

"Oh, you mean buyers of British arms?" *It was Ms Okereke.*

"That may be the Foreign Office's view, it's not mine. But either way, I need to take advice from our own lawyers."

"Minister, please. Tell us what the alternative is? Is it your intention to keep Adam here, alive, for the rest of his life? That would be unprecedented." *It was Doctor Atwan.*

"This man is accused of a serious crime. If he becomes competent, then he should be prosecuted."

"That's not going to happen, Minister. I will be happy to testify to that effect. In the courts. The humane thing is to let him go." *It was Doctor Atwan.*

"Like I say, I need to consult. And not just with Number 10. We might be sued by some of our largest companies. Like I say, there are tensions in the government. Where are the family? Don't they have a view?"

"Sir, they're not allowed to see Adam." *It was Dr Atwan.*

"What? Under whose authority?"

"Court of protection. It's a vulnerable adult case."

"Vulnerable adult? He's vulnerable to his own parents? My goodness, he can't move. What did they do? I thought they were good people when I met them?"

"We're not permitted to say, Sir." *It was Ms Okereke.*

"Give me strength. Okay, my first impression is it's a no. It's too early. I'll check with the lawyers, and if this has to go to the House Committee, then so be it. Either way, it's going to be a long wait. If you want to go to court, that's your prerogative. I won't stand in your way. But this needs due process and you are all too close to it."

"And you too, Minister?"

"You may be right, Doctor. I know you've been at the front line since the bomb went off. Well, I have too. We all had our battles to fight. Internally and externally. But we must remember how the outside world will see this. However we go forward, people will have seen those pictures in June. The carnage. The children he hurt. The innocent young woman who was wrongly blamed for murder. Whatever we say, they'll call him a criminal and whatever we decide, they'll want him to be punished."

"Thank you, Mr Gardiner. We understand. It's mostly out of all of our hands for now. He could pass away naturally, at any time, for all we know." *It was Doctor Atwan.*

Door.

"Well, that didn't go as well as we'd hoped."

"What do you think, Doctor Atwan?" *It was Dillon.*

"He's just blowing off steam. Didn't like being

confronted by all of us, especially with Adam in the room. To be honest, I don't think he has the authority to make a decision either way. He knows it'll be the Prime Minister, at the end of the day. If it comes to that."

"What would normally happen? I have to say, I'm not sure I've encountered anything like this?" *It was Ms Okereke.*

"There's not a lot of precedents. I've attended a few conferences, where papers have been presented about assisted dying for locked in patients. It's so hard, because there are so few cases, and not one case is the same.

"The doctors aren't even in agreement. Some claim the Hippocratic oath to preserve life and prevent harm overrides everything, even the patient's welfare. Others see the oath as irrelevant, once sentience has been absented. Add in a family that has directly opposed views, and the decision becomes even more complex. Who's in control then? The family? The doctors? What if there's a will? What if there's no will?"

"It's all so difficult." *It was Dillon.*

"And there's the added element of the Saudis. Extra pressure on the government." *It was Doctor Atwan.*

"Some of the court cases I've been involved with have gone on for years. The more complex, the longer it goes on. And this one's a beast." *It was Ms Okereke.*

"At the end of the day, everything can rest on a technicality. After all, Adam could still die at any time, and we'd avoid the courts completely. That way it could be different. Adam's life wouldn't be in question." *It was the doctor.*

Silence.

"In fact, in the name of acting humanely, there may be a way forward."

"I don't understand Doctor? What possible way forward is there?" *It was Dillon.*

Please don't give up on me, Dillon.

"What are you talking about Doctor?" *It was Ms Okereke.*

"The law. This hospital does not need permission to take away Adam's nutrition. At least, not now he's fed through an incision in his stomach. Do you remember? It doesn't need to go to court, as long as no next of kin or interested party objects.

"With the Pound family unable to make decisions about Adam, it falls to the medics only. And his current guardians: that's you, Mrs Okereke, with arguably Mr Kendrick too. We already have legal advice from Judge Millar to that effect. And now the Minister is threatening to question court decisions that don't go his way, I suspect Judge Millar may be cross enough to double down on his advice."

"Wow." *It was Ms Okereke.*

"I need to bring a medical colleague on board for a second opinion, probably the expert from York University Hospital who has followed this case. Together, we can decide whether our medical intervention is improving Adam's life chances, or his future quality of life. Clearly it's not, so..."

"So, you can remove the tube without court permission?" *It was Dillon.*

"Yes, if my colleague from York agrees. And I suspect even the government will find this is a nice little solution to their Saudi friends' desire for justice from the police. The Prime Minister will be able to keep the whole sorry affair at arm's length."

"So no courts, and no parents?" *It was Dillon.*

"Yes, just medicine. Professional, detached medicine. It's only the feeding through the mouth that is covered by rules that would force us to keep him alive."

"What are you saying Doctor?"

"What I'm saying is that I cannot - I will not - allow Adam to be held up as some pariah who deserves to be left in this state for the rest of his life. Things are more complex than that, we all know it."

35

Welcome to the evening Express News show, I'm Sophie Horgan.

This evening it has been revealed that the Saudi royal family has lobbied the UK government for the suspected London Pride bomber, Adam Pound, to be extradited to face justice in Riyadh. Our political editor, Natasha Harding, reports from outside the Foreign Office.

That's right, Sophie. I'm outside on a very cold night, here on Horse Guard's Parade, outside of the Foreign Office, where machinations have been taking place.

Mr Pound is strongly suspected by London's Metropolitan Police to have been responsible for the bomb, which killed 11 people, injured over one hundred others and left himself in a permanent coma. The man cannot be tried in the UK because he is in a permanent vegetative state, but the police have concluded that they are no longer looking for another perpetrator.

My understanding is that today, the Saudi royal family, who lost a relative in the bombing, has been demanding the

British government extradite Adam to their own judicial system, where a fair trial is promised.

Home Office Minister Francis Gardiner initially said this morning that the request could not be considered under human rights law, and there was no fixed extradition treaty between the two countries.

But later in the day, he seemed to slightly change his attitude, positing on Twitter that, I quote: 'The government does have the power to overrule courts, in the interest of British security.'

About half an hour ago, I picked up a statement from the Foreign Office, which I believe attempts to clarify the government's position. As I have said previously, it does seem as if the Home Office and the Foreign Office have been at odds on this matter.

In the statement, the Foreign Office Minister said that the case of Adam Pound was 'not one about the fate of a single terrorist, but about our wider national security which Saudi Arabia has long helped us to protect.'

He added: 'We have very clear signals from the hospital, that Adam Pound could possibly recover, and become aware. As such he needs to be kept alive in case he is then able to stand trial for his alleged crimes.'

Thank you, Natasha Harding. Has there been any response from the opposition?

Yes, there has. Even in the last hour, we've had Tweets and statements from the shadow Home Office minister, Red Wilson. He tweeted that 'Saudi Arabia routinely carries out human rights abuses and should not have any involvement in Adam Pound's case.'

Campaign group Human Rights Now said the very consideration of a comatose man standing trial in a state which is wholly controlled by a single family, and has no independent democracy or judicial system, is unacceptable and puts the British government to shame.

I attempted to put this to a government spokesperson, but was unable to get a response. In a personal Tweet, the Home Office minister, Francis Gardiner said 'My government will not get involved in lazy speculation.'

Natasha, can you give your analysis on these events?

Well, it is very early and this issue will run and run. The way I see it diplomatically is that the Prime Minister and the Home Secretary are in a very difficult situation in opposition to the Foreign Office. The question of extraditing a comatose man to any country is unthinkable, but the power of the Saudi royal family and its special relationship with the UK, particularly in arms and oil, is not insignificant.

At the very least, Ministers will want to keep Adam Pound alive long enough to see an official inquiry lay the blame for the bombing on Adam Pound's shoulders. That's as good as a conviction, in the public's eyes, and may open the door for further action against Mr Pound if he ever recovers.

Could Adam be realistically sent to Saudi Arabia? It seems unlikely, but these are very complex circumstances, with a member of the Saudi royal family still being very publicly mourned in the streets of Riyadh.

Thank you Natasha Harding. And here in the studio, we have our legal correspondent Hamish Lee who has been following the case of Adam Pound closely.

Yes, Sophie, my understanding is that it has become a somewhat ugly race for time, doctors are taking legal advice as to whether to allow Mr Pound to die. They argue this is because they say he has no chance of recovering or improving in his condition, and it is the kindest thing to do.

Meantime, minsters are considering whether to launch a court stay against allowing him to die, until the inquiry into the bombing is completed. Normally, the parents of Adam Pound would have a strong sway either way, but their responsibility for decisions about Mr Pound has been stripped away because of historical allegations and Adam Pound's vulnerability.

Adam Pound's natural passing away might be most convenient for doctors and, possibly the government in the long term. But the Saudis are likely to see his not standing trial at all as a betrayal of their relationship with Britain.

Thank you Hamish Lee. In other news...

36

Door.

"Oh, Adam. I don't know if this is the right thing to do."

Dillon?

"I shouldn't be here. They've brought you into a private ICU room. Doctor Atwan will be along soon. She said she would overlook my coming here, but she doesn't know what I'm about to do. What I'm about to ask of you."

It's okay. Tell me what you're going to do.

"Listen, before I ask the question, I just want to let you know something. From the bottom of my heart."

I love you too, Dillon.

"It wasn't your fault. I'm sorry for doubting it. I'm sorry for going away. I needed to get my head straight. I felt guilty, you know? I felt bad because I'd supported you all these months and, well, it turned out this way."

You're not to blame, Dillon. What do you want to ask me?

"But then I got to see. You know, through all the talk, and the vitriol, I realised that people want someone to blame. An easy answer. It's not enough that things just happen, is it? That sometimes, occasionally, the world is a shit place, full of shit people, with shit backgrounds, and poor support, and poor mental health, and bullies, and crap parents."

"Poor Adam, abused by his folks. Rejected by his dad. Growing up gay, when it was the last thing you needed in your life. You were not to blame. It was so much more complex. So I blamed myself. If only I could have prevented it. If I had met you before. Made you feel okay to be gay. I could have stopped this. This whole thing."

Don't cry. I'm here for you. It's not your fault.

"You are someone who never got a chance. Someone who has suffered all their life, at the hands of a warped church that punishes, and whips, and burns those within its care. To me, that is what you are. I did my job."

Hold me Dillon.

"Adam, the doctor will come soon. She can't know I've come early. She shouldn't know what I'm about to do."

Is this real? Are you going to ask what I think you are?

"This isn't supposed to happen at all, like breaking ethical rules. But hey. This is the only chance we've got."

Dillon, what are you saying? Are you going to ask to marry me?

"Given the circumstances, I want to share some of my life with you. After all, I know so much about you, but you know nothing about me."

Oh, Dillon, you can share all of your life with me.

"Anyway, if this is my last chance, I know it's rather selfish of me because I'll get what I want. But wait, just wait one moment, I need to check for the doctor."

Oh, tell me you're going to marry me. Even if it's just you and me, right now, in this room. I can't wait any longer.

Door.

"Quickly, come in."

Dillon?

"Adam, I want you to meet Tammy. She's my wife. She's the biggest part of my life. And I wanted you to, well, to know her."

"Hello Adam. Is that right? Should I talk to him directly? I'm pleased to meet you, Adam."

Wife, Dillon? Oh, God. No! How could you! No, oh God no.

"I've heard so much about you, Adam. We wanted to say thank you. You've done so much for Dillon. He's, well, he's gained a lot from this experience. We're so proud of him."

Wife? I don't understand. That can't be Dillon. Oh, I feel sick. I thought we were together Dillon. You and me?

"Adam, me and Tammy have been together for three years. We got married last year."

Married! You were going to marry me. No, this isn't right. This isn't real. Damn you.

"Is he okay, Dillon?"

"Yes, he's fine."

I am not fine. You told me you were gay. I'm sure you did. How dare you? Who is she? Why didn't you tell me, Dillon? You let me... I can't stand it. You let me fall in love with you. Oh, my God. Oh what a mess. What a mistake.

"I hope you're happy Adam. I so wish you could be with us, to share this moment with us.

"Oh, Dillon." *It was Tammy.*

Silence.

Crying.

Dillon crying?

"It's okay, you know. I know you love him. It's okay. I understand." *It was Tammy.*

Do you, Dillon?

"You understand?"

"How can you not? You two have been through so much together, and I've watched you so closely. And do you know what? I love you all the more for it. It's going to be okay." *It was Tammy.*

Crying.

And now I'm crying, Dillon. I know I can never have you. I'm so sad, but I know I can never have you. You need to be with your wife. Please. I never deserved his love.

Silence.

"Tam, do you still want to..."

"Yes, yes of course. We should share it with him."

Share?

"Okay. Should I say it?"

Say what, Dillon?

"Come here, let me wipe your tears away first."

Silence.

"Okay? Adam, we wanted you to know. We're expecting a baby."

What?

"We're going to call her Daisy. The midwife said she was a girl." *It was Dillon.*

A baby, Dillon? A child?

Silence.

Oh, how wonderful. God, I hurt, but how wonderful. Dillon, you will be happy. You will have a sweet, beautiful baby girl. Oh, I cannot be sad for myself, when you could be so happy. Finally, Dillon, I can let you go. Into the arms of someone who loves you. And someone who will love you from the moment they are born.

"Dillon, you're crying again?" *It was Tammy.*

"I hope you're happy for us Adam. I so wish you could be with us right now."

I am here. Oh my Dillon, oh Tammy, oh Daisy. I'm so, so

happy for you. I deserve nothing but hate. But you've shown me so much love.

"Adam, I hope you feel this is right. I don't know, but we've talked about it, Tammy and I. You see, I know you are a Christian and that must have meant so much to you. And even if you're not, well..."

Tell me.

"We'd like you to bless our baby, Adam." *It was Dillon.*

Oh, my God. I don't deserve this. You should hate me. I'm not worth this.

"Adam, I'm holding your hand against my tummy now. It feels so warm. So gentle. I wish you could feel her. Ah, she's kicking right now."

"Kicking?" *It was Dillon.*

"Go on, put your hand over her too. We can all share her, just for a moment."

Oh, I don't deserve this.

"Ah, I can feel it. It's amazing."

I wish I could feel her. But I can imagine it. I can imagine it!

"Maybe we should be quiet for a moment?" *It was Tammy.*

Silence.

God, I hope you can hear me. I don't know what to call you anymore. Perhaps you are the stars, and the sun, and the universe, and everything beautiful in the world. Before you once again engulf me, I hope you will bless this baby Daisy. She deserves the best chance. She deserves all the joy you can bring her. Make her safe and happy. Let her life be as free from harm and hurt as anyone could ask for. If it is worth anything, that is my dying wish. Please, bless this child. And allow me to go to hell, where I belong.

Silence.

Crying.

"Look at us." *It was Dillon.*

"Come on, you lovely sensitive man. Let's get you cleaned up before the doctor arrives. Adam, thank you. With all of our hearts, thank you. We will never forget this moment."

37

Door.

"Dillon, come in."

"Thank you, Doctor Atwan"

"Please, call me Lopa. It's my Yemeni name. I think it's time you did."

"Lopa."

Lopa, what a beautiful name.

"How do you feel?" *It was Lopa.*

"Nervous. But I know it's the right thing."

"Let me prepare."

"What should I do?"

"Hold his hand, perhaps. For your own sake?"

What are you preparing Lopa? I hope it is what I'm wishing for.

"Do you think they loved him?"

"His parents?"

"Well, his dad."

"What parent doesn't love their child? But his dad had baggage. A whole lot of warped baggage. He's not safe around Adam, he never was."

"Geoff Pound's own dad did it to him, you know. You saw the limp."

"I did. What chance did Geoff Pound have to be a good father. The influence of our parents. The church. The communities we belong to."

"Doctor, do you think we really have choice in who we become? Like, can we ever escape our influences?"

"Well, I'm a Doctor because my parents wanted me to be. It was their ambitions I was living out, not mine. Of course, I'm glad now. But twenty years ago? I wanted to be a musician, or a dancer, or anything where I didn't have to work hard."

"All those things require hard work." *It was Dillon.*

"Yes, I suppose you're right. Are you ready?"

"Are you sure, Lopa?"

"I'm sure as I'll ever be. Which is not very sure. But I am a doctor, I care about my patients, and I hope that I know best."

"And might there be, I mean, could you get in trouble? Could we get in trouble?"

"His passing away has been very possible at any stage. By removing his feeding, I'm only allowing that process that would happen anyway at some point. I have the official backing of my medical colleagues."

"You are a good person, Lopa."

"No, I'm a good doctor. I do what I have to do in my patients' longer term interests. The media will move on. Many will be secretly pleased. An issue solved. The Saudis will settle. The Home Office will breathe again. Adam's family will be able to grieve, unashamed."

It's okay, Dillion. You can let me go. Don't worry now.

"And you, Doctor?"

"I will stand by my professional judgement. It will be

questioned, but that is part of medicine. I think most will be sympathetic in the end."

"And you, personally."

"Dillon, I deal with death every day. Each one is sad, but it's part of life. We all need to live our truth. I live mine as a doctor. Adam wasn't able to live his, nor his father."

I can live my truth now, Dillon. You've given me the greatest gift.

"It'll take a few weeks. But we'll take him down to our End of Life ward. They'll take really good care of him. Any final words? I can leave the room if you like?"

"No, it's okay Doctor. I've said everything I have to say."

And I too, Dillon. Goodnight my sweet, sweet man.

Silence.

Dear Valued Reader,

Thank you for reading this book.

I hope you have been entertained, perhaps challenged and that you would like to read more of my writing.

You can find out more about my books at
www.gideon-burrows.com

It would make a real difference to me if you were able to please leave a **review** on your **social media**, share your **recommendation** with your friends, and please write an honest review on your **favourite book buying and review site**.

I have a free book for you, if you sign up to my monthly newsletter. Simply go to my website to get it.

Thank you again for reading!
Gideon Burrows
www.gideon-burrows.com

CLAIM YOUR FREE BOOK

Rosa Bodran is in a rush as usual.

The ferocious weather is doing everything it can to prevent her getting on with her day.

A strange man offers her a virtual reality shopping experience, guaranteeing it will be quicker, easier and cheaper than her usual family shop.

It'll mean she can pick up her kids on time, despite the freezing hail and wind.

But all is not as it seems.

Futuristic shopping might not be the solution to Rosa's problems.

It could put everything she cares for at risk.

Dive into this mystery futurist thriller, and face some of the deepest questions about how you want your own future to look.

From the award winning author of Portico and The Illustrator's

Daughter, comes a short book that shows this challenging writer at the cutting edge of what he does.

Get FREE direct from the author

THE ILLUSTRATOR'S DAUGHTER

What is any parent's greatest fear?

In a beautiful way it explores the story of a family which is facing some very hard times and helps ask difficult questions about how we would react under similar circumstances. *****

A brilliant book. Couldn't put it down *****

This book took my breath away. Absolutely couldn't put it down. Beautifully written, it explores some hugely emotional issues with honesty and grace. *****

Honest, heartbreaking and unputdownable *****

Loving parents. A brand new baby girl. They should have been an ideal young family.

It doesn't always turn out that way.

Matt Carron is desperate not to lose his perfect wife, but he can't hide his jealousy when his daughter is born.

As Minnie becomes a toddler, he's driven crazy by her tantrums. When she gets a jigsaw wrong. When she won't listen or won't eat.

When he has to pin her to the ground so hard she bruises her arms.

When Minnie becomes seriously ill, the family embarks on a desperate mission to understand the condition and its treatment.

But the couple have very different ideas about what will work, driving a gap between them so severe it could mean life or death for their daughter.

Can Matt finally comes to terms with the unbearable choice he's been avoiding for twelve years?

His daughter or his wife?

The Illustrator's Daughter is a heart-wrenching novel about the deep challenges all of our relationships might face, living with the decisions we make, and choosing between unbearable futures.

Please buy direct from the author

ACKNOWLEDGMENTS

The most difficult parts of this book were written during a very cold January week, when I took advantage of my wife's generosity and hid myself away in a hotel on the coast. I left her to look after the children alone. It could not have happened without that head space, so thank you to her and the rest of my family.

I offer my grateful thanks to Newham Writers' Workshop, my new found friends in writing. Together they have looked over parts of the book, and always offered me generous praise and constructive criticism. Thanks to Paula Smith and Paul Butler especially for giving the book a forensic critique.

Thanks also to Kay Barrett for eagle eye proofreading, and to my regular Alpha and Beta readers for giving the book a look over. Any remaining errors are entirely my own.

Printed in Great Britain
by Amazon